LIFE ON THIS PLANET
and Other Stories

LIFE ON THIS PLANET
and Other Stories

MATT COHEN

BEAUFORT BOOKS
Publishers · New York

No character in this book is intended to represent any actual person; all the incidents of the story are entirely fictional in nature.

Copyright © 1979, 1980, 1981, 1983 by Matt Cohen

All rights reserved. No part of this publication may be reproduced or transmitted in any form or by any means, electronic or mechanical, including photocopy, recording, or any information storage and retrieval system now known or to be invented, without permission in writing from the publisher, except by a reviewer who wishes to quote brief passages in connection with a review written for inclusion in a magazine, newspaper, or broadcast.

Library of Congress Cataloging-in-Publication Data

Cohen, Matt, 1942-
Life on this planet, and other stories.
I. Title.
PR9199.3.C58L5 1985   813'.54   85-9059
ISBN 0-8253-0313-3

Published in the United States by Beaufort Books Publishers, New York.
Originally published as *Café le Dog* in Canada,
by McClelland and Stewart Limited.

Printed in the U.S.A.   First American Edition

10 9 8 7 6 5 4 3 2 1

Acknowledgements

Some of these stories have appeared in *The Canadian Fiction Magazine*, *The Malahat Review*, and *The North American Review*. "Sentimental Meetings" is to be broadcast on CBC *Anthology*.

Contents

Golden Whore of the Heartland   9
Life on This Planet   61
The Sins of Tomas Benares   76
Death of a Guppy   103
Sentimental Meetings   114
A Love for the Infinite   131
At the Empress Hotel   141
Café Le Dog · 165

Golden Whore of the Heartland

Malcolm Totting tried to kill himself by swallowing sleeping pills – two dozen of them one afternoon before Benton was to arrive in order to pick Totting up for dinner. When Benton got to the door, it was open. Totting had left a note on the dining room table saying that he was lying dead in the bedroom. He was extremely sorry to have burdened Benton with such a task, but could he call the police and an ambulance before his body began to smell. The note went on to say that his affairs were all in order, the will written and recently updated, and that the refrigerator had been defrosted by the cleaning lady. It was signed, "With all best wishes, Malcolm Totting," and there was a postscript giving the relevant telephone numbers.

After supervising Totting's trip to the hospital, Benton went downtown to the restaurant where they were to have eaten, and sat in the bar drinking one scotch after another. When he was too drunk to drive he telephoned his wife to explain why he was going to sleep over at Totting's apartment. Then he returned to the bar where he saw a table of his favourite graduate students. After two more doubles Thalia Stewart asked him if anything was wrong.

"I stayed in town because my car broke down."

"I'll drive you home if you like," she said.

"I think I'll have another drink."

"The bar closed half an hour ago." Her voice was a loud whisper, as if she was speaking through a megaphone. Benton remembered going out to her car, winking at the other students as he climbed into the front seat. She was already on the expressway, driving towards the farm he had described often enough to his class, when he told her that he was staying in town that night, at Malcolm Totting's.

As he stepped out of the car he stumbled and fell on his face. It was a unique sensation: first there was the long, dizzy moment when he knew his balance was lost; next came the urgent but ever-more-useless effort to regain it; and finally, the best part – the long, slow, swoon that ended only when his face and stomach landed in Malcolm Totting's parking space. Fortunately it had been raining all night. Benton made a harmless landing into the wet mud.

"I'll help you upstairs," Thalia offered.

"I'm okay."

But he stumbled again. Thalia had to link her arm through his, she was amazingly strong for such a thin and awkward girl, and push him through the lobby and into the elevator. After opening Totting's door and guiding him to the bathroom where he splashed off the mud, Thalia steered Robert Benton along the hall to Malcolm's bedroom. Standing at the foot of the bed, he noticed that the bedspread still held the imprint of Malcolm's drugged body. Then he passed out. When he woke up he was completely lucid, naked under the covers, his arm wrapped protectively around the equally naked body of Thalia Stewart, to whom he had given a B plus on her most recent essay. Her skin was taut and warm, and as he moved his hand along her ribs Benton could feel the soft, vulnerable drumming of her heart. Her face was turned towards him. She was smiling in her sleep. Benton's first thought was that he hoped Thalia hadn't seen the note on the dining room table.

Benton got out of bed, feeling quite free to wander naked into Malcolm's dining room. The note was on the table.

Scribbled at the bottom was a new postscript, "He's all right, but he has to spend a week in hospital – TS."

There was a brief moment in which Benton realized there was still time to rescue his marriage. "Sometimes you have to decide," Totting had said to him only a few weeks ago, "which you are going to save – your marriage or your life." Benton went back to the bedroom and slid beneath the covers. Thalia's body searched out his own, and as he wrapped his arms around her slender back, he couldn't help wondering if Thalia had been Malcolm's mistress too.

The afternoon Thalia announced that she was pregnant, Benton was still living with his wife. He advised Thalia to have the abortion and then finish her thesis.

"Who needs another thesis on Blake. And I won't have anything truly original unless I go to England."

"You should go to England," Benton said. He meant it; he even dared to hope that her love for him would survive the separation and that they would be joined together in a misty future. "While you're gone I can straighten out my own situation."

"I'll go," Thalia offered. "But I can't have an abortion."

"Why not?"

"I don't believe in it," she said, with such determination that Benton, twenty years older than her, suddenly felt that all of his own convictions had been bargained away in a series of compromises too boring to recount.

A year later, Benton was divorced from his wife, and Thalia was in place with the baby at the farm outside of Toronto. "I've never lived on the land," she said. "Never really lived *on* it." As if she had spent her whole life floating above the ground and now wanted to come, literally, down to earth.

"You know," Benton said, "you really *believe* what you say."

"Don't you believe what *you* say?"

"Of course," Benton protested, wondering which of his declarations of love and lifelong fidelity she was now reviewing, "I believe what I say but, you know, I feel that my life has been so sordid –"

"You like to believe your life has been sordid. You read about F. Scott Fitzgerald too much."

"Too much, too soon," Benton murmured.

"You're really a very conservative man," Thalia declared. "I know you've never had a dishonourable thought in your life."

Thalia became the second woman to live with Benton in the white frame farmhouse that Benton himself had rebuilt. But as Benton had explained to Thalia, what really counted to him was not the house but what surrounded it. Over the years the topography of his farm had become the living and breathing map of his own body: its dank depressions, its brief moments of glory, its little nooks of life that existed in defiance of larger forces – these were all so essential to him that he needed to travel over them almost daily in order to believe he was still alive.

The farm itself was located forty miles from downtown Toronto. At night the lights of the city sent a glow through the southern portion of the sky, so that Benton always felt, no matter how deeply he wandered into the surrounding woods and hills, that he was only the blink of an eye from the city's perpetually humming downtown.

"I love it here," Thalia said one night. "While you're at the university I look out the window and imagine that Jonah and I live here all alone, a hundred years ago."

Thalia made this welcome announcement while they were getting ready for bed. During Thalia's first weekend at the house, Benton had told her its one hundred and forty years of history, including the story of how the wife of the farmer who'd built the house had died, in this very bedroom, during the birth of her fifth child.

"But the child lived," Benton had rushed on to say, "and he was the one who kept the farm. Built the big barn out by the pond and drained off the marsh so it could be used for hay and wheat."

Thalia, pregnant with Jonah, had nodded with what seemed to be boredom, and Benton had been embarrassed with his own moralizing.

But now that Thalia was firmly installed as mistress of the house, Benton found himself suspiciously close to contentment. Warm and secure, he lay under the down comforter with Thalia's head resting on his shoulder, her voice reassuring in his ear. She was, in fact, just telling him once again how much she enjoyed her days when Benton began to hear, along with the sound of the wind scraping along the metal siding he himself had applied, the convulsive shudder that the oil furnace made when the chimney draft stayed open.

"Christ."

"What? Is it silly for me to be happy here?"

"It's wonderful. I meant that the draft is stuck again. I'd better go fix it."

"Cold," Thalia said.

"I'll go." But he hesitated. The basement had a dirt floor with the massive furnace – an old woodburner converted to oil in honour of the young and tender flesh of both Jonah and Thalia – set up on a cement pedestal. The single lightbulb that was suspended from the stairs threw shadows of old beams and twisted nails around the stone walls; and sometimes Benton wanted to laugh at himself for the additional shapes his eyes invented.

"Leave it," Thalia said. "What's the difference?"

Benton switched on the bedside lamp and saw his own enormous shadow spring up on the bedroom wall. "It's crazy," he said, "I know. But I hate to see that perfectly good oil going up the chimney. Don't you think I should fix it?"

"You should. I mean you should fix it so that you don't have to go down there every time the wind blows." Benton, pulling on his housecoat, couldn't help noticing the way Thalia was starting to imitate his patterns of speech.

The next day, after teaching his Wednesday class in American fiction, Benton was making a list of all the minor chores he had neglected for months when Robyn Marler stepped into his office and closed the door behind her.

The day he first saw her, the previous September, he thought she was part of the year's crop of graduate students. She wore high-heeled shoes that emphasized her tightly-skirted legs, and when she walked she switched, like a nervous filly, the long golden hair that hung halfway down the back of her carefully tailored suit.

"Do you mind if I come in?" Robyn asked.

"Of course not."

Robyn Marler *was* a newcomer to the Department, but not a graduate student: in her forties she had a slender, almost steely, body, and a prim, upright neck leading to a lined and weathered face which was undeniably a record of the dissipation which was her academic specialty. That is, she had written a book about Coleridge and Wordsworth in which she claimed that Coleridge was the greater poet because he was willing to burn his brains out on drugs, while Wordsworth confined himself to the stimulation of the damp countryside and his sister's incestuous ministrations.

This book, which Benton had somehow read even before Marler was invited to be Visiting Professor, had been published by a prestigious American house, and was translated into enough languages to use up two lines of her *curriculum vitae*.

Marler sat in the student visiting chair, crossed her legs, and lit a cigarette.

"Terrible weather," Benton said. "It doesn't always get this bad."

"I never go outside," replied Marler. "Except for walks. I take a walk every day."

"So do I," Benton said. It was easy to imagine Robyn Marler walking. With her brisk stride, smoking non-stop, she would whip herself up and down the streets until she returned exhausted to her apartment. He could imagine the apartment, too, because it was sublet from Malcolm Totting who had risen from the ashes of his unsuccessful suicide to be awarded a sabbatical, springing free not only the apartment, but also the salary and the office that the renowned Robyn Marler was now occupying.

"The thing is," Marler said, "if you don't mind me getting to it . . . "

"Go ahead."

"I want to stay on after this year, and I was wondering if you could tell me how."

Benton blushed, a sudden flash of heat rushing through him as if he had just seen Robyn Marler in a ridiculous and obscene position.

"Why," Benton finally asked, "why would someone like you want to stay in Canada? Don't you feel cut off from – "

"One of my students," Marler explained. "I've fallen in love. He's only in second year and I don't think he's smart enough to change universities . . ."

Benton felt his blush grow yet deeper. Then he saw that Robyn Marler was starting to grin.

"Sorry," she giggled, "I never learned to tell the truth. You didn't believe me, did you?" She laughed.

Benton found himself laughing, too.

"Actually, I just came by to see if you'd join me for lunch."

She laughed again, her laugh extending itself into a surprising little-girl giggle, and Benton couldn't help laughing with her.

By the time Benton got home the sun had already set, leaving only a thin red souvenir along the horizon. As soon as he got out of the car, Benton set out on his walk, running from the driveway to the road so that Thalia wouldn't have a chance to shout to him.

Once over the first hill and out of sight of the house, he slowed rapidly. His breath was irregular and choking; the three scotches he had drunk with Robyn Marler threatened to make their own dash for freedom.

Shouldn't drink, he admonished himself. *I know I shouldn't drink.* Three years previously, on his fortieth birthday, Benton had found out that he had a mild case of diabetes; nothing serious the doctor had said then, Benton's only symptom being persistent fatigue.

"It's all right," Benton said. "F. Scott Fitzgerald had diabetes. His doctor told him not to drink, too."

"Who's he?"

"I don't know. I guess I could look it up. No one ever asked me that before – who was the doctor of F. Scott Fitzgerald?"

"No," Benton's doctor said gently, "I didn't mean who was the doctor."

"A writer," Benton said. "Fitzgerald. They made movies out of his books. I teach a course on him."

"*The Great Gatsby*," the doctor suddenly supplied.

"That's it."

"He was an alcoholic, wasn't he?"

"I'm not," Benton said, suddenly irritated, his mind filled with a picture of Fitzgerald sitting in an airplane toilet, drunkenly trying to force a syringe into his thigh. "Will I have to take insulin?"

"Exercise and diet."

Two miles from the house Benton was sober again, and he turned around to go home. Thalia would be waiting for him, supper made in one of the copper pots he had given her last Christmas. Benton realized he had forgotten to eat lunch. He reached into a pocket for a cigarette, then began walking again, trying to imagine now what would happen if he invited Robyn out for dinner. She didn't have a car, he remembered her saying; she would have to stay overnight.

Near the house, Benton stopped and looked over a rocky hill to a barn that had been gradually falling down, walls buckling a foot at a time, for the entire ten years he had lived on the farm. He realized he had been thinking that Thalia would be jealous of Robyn, because Robyn was an active and independent woman with a career of her own while Thalia, once a pretty and awkward girl with a halo of scholarships and a promising academic future, had under Benton's care evolved into a beautiful and somewhat bored young woman who looked after a baby and tried to remember to work on her thesis in her spare time.

"You know," Robyn Marler said, "you really are an extraordinary person to be buried away in a place like this."

"And where," Benton asked, "should my light be shining?" They had developed the habit of a daily visit to report on departmental gossip, commiserate on the stupidity of students and bureaucrats, and smoke one another's cigarettes.

In fact, Benton thought, the compulsive smoking of each other's cigarettes was a pervasive theme, a clear line that extended so markedly through their meetings that it deserved special mention – a term paper, or perhaps a thesis: "Oral Substitution and Sublimation as Practised by the Department of English." But, the question was, for what were the cigarettes a substitute? Because although Benton enjoyed the idea that they were putting bits of each other into their mouths, he had no desire to touch or kiss or, even less, taste the actual parts of Robyn Marler. With her lined face, the colour of seasoned oak, and her thin, stringy-looking hands, she gave the impression that beneath her concealing and smartly-tailored clothes was the sinewy body of a cat grown past catting. Robyn Marler was, as Benton had explained to Thalia, not only a cat grown past catting, but a single woman past the point of being on the make. There was, Benton said, no word for her at all. With her dyed-blonde hair, her fingers smoked to the colour of kippers by her filterless cigarettes, her tense movements and flashy smile, she had reached a strange no-woman's land between spinster and dame.

"Your intense light?" Robyn asked, in a tone that was beginning to make Benton feel slightly uncomfortable. Then she shrugged her shoulders. "That's the problem these days. It's easy to hate where we are; but there's nowhere worth lusting after."

"It's not so bad here," Benton said.

"No, it isn't really." She reached, they were in Benton's office, for one of Benton's cigarettes. He couldn't help noticing that her fingers were cleaner today, as if they had been pumiced. According to her *curriculum vitae* Robyn was forty-six years old, only three years older than himself. But every time he found his eyes riveted on her masculine hands, the unsuggestive lines of her suit, the tiny but intricately detailed pouches under her eyes, he couldn't help feeling guilty about inspecting his new friend this way. Especially guilty, he knew, because he assumed that Robyn was sexually desperate enough to regard him as an attractive male, even if his light was placed under a provincial bushel. In fact, from feeling like a pariah at the beginning of the year, Benton had progressed, under Robyn's encouraging gaze and her carefully dropped comments, to being convinced he was almost respectable. Of course he was not going to win a popularity contest, though that defeat – in such surroundings – was no serious wound. But he *was* liked and sought after by graduate students, the prettiest and most intelligent of which he had somehow captured on a full-time basis; he had tenure, and was paid a large salary to work a few hours a week for eight months of the year; he was known for his professional competence; and his University Press book on F. Scott Fitzgerald, although not translated, still earned occasional praise for its elegance of style and its sympathetic understanding of Fitzgerald's passive character.

"And anyway," Benton said, "*you* came here. That says something for us." The Department had been pleasantly shocked when its Chairman, returning from a conference in Los Angeles, intimated that the Visiting Chair might be occupied by Robyn Marler, the distinguished Coleridgean who was on a leave of absence from Princeton. Before she arrived, there had been jokes that Robyn Marler and the Chairman must have conceived one of those unlikely convention passions where Circe melts even the stiffest of Puritanical collars.

"I didn't mean to sound ungrateful."

"Ungrateful," Benton said. "It's *we* who should be grateful. Why would you want to spend a year in Toronto when you might have been in England, Europe . . ." He cut himself off, realizing that he had done it, asked the question he had promised himself to avoid because it was obvious to him and everyone else that Robyn Marler must have chosen to spend a year in Canada either because she was financially distressed beyond the need for an ordinary prestigious fellowship – which surely she could have had – or because her stress was an emotional one and she needed, after the well-publicized death of her well-publicized husband, a place where she could both hide and be looked after, a refuge which wasn't lonely, a sort of benevolent mental institution.

"You see," Robyn said, her voice still flat, "I had a . . . disagreement . . . with the Dean while my husband was ill." Hugh Walpole Marler had been notorious for the wonderfully malevolent cartoons he had drawn for the *New York Times Book Review*. Whenever a book was to be panned, Marler was employed to sketch the author in a state of dementia. When he discovered he had terminal cancer he wrote an article saying that approaching death made him realize that the hatred he had exercised on various writers had so poisoned his heart that he felt absolutely indifferent to everyone, even his own family.

"Anyone can disagree," Benton said.

"It wasn't a disagreement on policy matters. It was more of a personal confrontation. He didn't actually fire me, I should say. What happened was that I offered my resignation, and he accepted it."

Robyn lit a new cigarette while her first was still smoking, and her hands moved with such agitation that Benton was sure he was about to hear a story that he didn't want the burden of knowing.

"That was that," Robyn said. "I wasn't joking when I said I'd like to stay. But since then I've been offered another job. An old friend in Pennsylvania." She stood up and quickly brushed her hand through her dyed-blonde hair. The gesture was so unusual and girlish that Benton also sprang to his feet.

"We should go to lunch," Benton said.

"I'm going home," Robyn replied. "I have to prepare for a seminar this afternoon. And anyway, I'm afraid I'd be depressing company today."

"Don't be silly." Benton began to panic at the thought of Robyn, depressed, in Totting's apartment. "I absolutely insist."

"No, really, *I* absolutely insist." For a moment Robyn looked at him, her smile beginning to flash as it did when she was about to make one of her off-putting remarks. But her lips only parted sadly, and then she gave a smile of such vulnerable sweetness that Benton was paralyzed. Before he could speak, Robyn was out of the office and into the hall, her boots on the marble floor melting quickly into the Department's lunchtime rush to the Faculty Club.

"You see," Benton explained to Thalia, "she's amazingly vulnerable. It must have taken a lot of courage for her to move here."

"You should invite her out," Thalia said. "She must be terribly lonely so close to Christmas."

"Dinner would be nice," Benton said.

"Why not have her for the weekend?" Thalia asked. "All you do these days is mark papers. I wouldn't mind the company and you could use an excuse to rest. I'm worried about you." She got up from her chair and stood solicitously beside him, putting her palm on his forehead as if to test his temperature. Jonah, who was trying out a highchair for the first time, threw his apple sauce on the floor and screamed. Thalia bent over and kissed Benton: once, twice. It was the way, he remembered, that she used to lean over and kiss him the week they stayed at Totting's apartment, making love and visiting Malcolm at the hospital. Thalia had not been, it turned out, Totting's lover; in fact she had never been anyone's lover at all. "I saved my whole life for you."

"You shouldn't say those things."

"They're true."

That night Benton woke up in a sweat. He put on his dressing gown but the nervous sweat kept flowing like a river down his backbone, dampening the crack between his buttocks, making him shiver as if he were starting the flu.

The furnace was rattling away but that wasn't the problem: he had been dreaming about the kiss Thalia had given him at the supper table, the full press of her lips against his own. But in his dream the lips had belonged to the sad, wise, mouth of Robyn Marler. Thalia had been a virgin but

Robyn, Benton knew, was anything but. In the dream he had felt himself, like a hippopotamus sinking gratefully into soft mud, diving happily into the total corruption of Robyn Marler; with her honey-blonde golden whore hair and her wise-dirty smile she embraced and drew him into the sweet drugged heartland of New York vice and corruption. And in fact those very words, golden whore of the heartland, had been on his tongue as he, dreaming, returned Robyn's kiss and pressed himself eagerly against her – already wondering what the neighbours would say when Thalia and Jonah disappeared, were replaced by this aging American goddess redolent of the thousands of bodies that had eagerly lusted after her.

Benton went downstairs to the living room and poured himself a glass of brandy. The truth was, he now accused himself, that he had known from the very moment Robyn Marler had walked into his office six weeks ago that he was going to sleep with her, that he was going to have an affair with her that might or might not be sweet but would certainly be guilt-ridden and would certainly wrench him away from Thalia; and he also had known, he now forced himself to admit, that this affair would be as unpleasant for Robyn as it would be for himself, that she and Thalia would both be wounded, possibly even destroyed.

"But why," Benton said aloud. "*Why bother?*" He had poured himself a second drink and was dialling the number of his own true friend, Malcolm Totting, when he realized the call would be answered not by Malcolm but by Robyn.

"Jesus," Benton said, hanging up the receiver.

It would have happened, he realized, on this very day if he had offered to take Robyn home. Not only was her apartment Malcolm's, but it was also the scene of his initial tryst with Thalia. And, to tell the truth, there had been a few times in his married years when parties at Malcolm's had ended with himself and one woman or another sleeping it off on Malcolm's capacious Victorian couch.

Maybe, he suddenly thought, it was a psychological thing, a need to defy his own best friend. "I am not," Benton had once shouted, filled with derision for his wife, "a member of the human potential movement! What most shrinks need is a good crap."

The brandy began to settle in his stomach and Benton began to settle also; gradually, the dream was replaced by the comforting view of the room he had lived in these past ten years, the books he had read and placed into the shelves his hands had awkwardly made. It wasn't true, he said to himself; Robyn didn't want him and he didn't want her. It was natural for adults to be sympathetic to and interested in each other. Such a minor attraction – one which was really a repulsion – didn't have to pull him into a *danse macabre* that would destroy his life.

And as he reassured himself and lit a cigarette, another disturbing idea flitted by: he didn't have to worry, he could change wives, change houses, even change medical regimes and it wouldn't matter – it didn't threaten his life at all, it barely even affected it.

Benton stood up and walked to the window. The dark glass threw back his own reflection, and despite everything he looked tall and thin, as fit as he had been twenty years ago. The whole autumn he had walked as the doctor prescribed, and had confined his drinking to the social minimum. The complaints he once had – fatigue and occasional dizziness – had entirely disappeared. He remembered thinking that he was going to die because it would be unfair to live past the lifespan of the person from whom he had made his money. But now, at forty-three, he was older than F. Scott Fitzgerald had ever been. "He died not of drink but of work," Benton had written in his biography, a book that portrayed F. Scott Fitzgerald not as the madcap alcoholic Zelda wanted him to be, but as a man whose sincere desire to stick to his last had been corrupted – but only temporarily – by desire. The desire for fame, for the touch of beautiful women, the release of alcohol, and, most of all, the drunkenness of love.

Now, in his living room, Benton remembered how clearly he had understood that love was corrupting and evil. This understanding, fuelled by his frequent separations from his wife, had pushed him through draft after draft of the Fitzgerald book. "It must be a work of love," Totting joked once. "No," Benton protested, "it's only hate."

Benton poured himself a third brandy. It was amazing the way a man could drift away from himself. Benton stood up again, so pleased to be remembering his own lessons that he couldn't help pacing the room. Outside he now saw a car driving by, its white headlights scanning the snowbanks. For a moment Benton was afraid that it was lost and in trouble, and was going to turn up his own driveway. But it went on, slowly following the road that led only to the houses of a few farmers who had to get up at five in the morning to do the milking. *It must be a doctor*, Benton thought. *Someone must be sick*. He started towards the hall, as if he would go upstairs and get dressed, ready to help. But he was too drunk, he had lost touch with who was sick and who was well, and if Thalia knew these things, as his wife used to in intricate detail, she did not pass the information on to him.

But even the car, like a stranger walking through his own living room, could not shatter Benton's feeling that for once the world was in its place.

The weekend, to begin with, was a disaster. Thalia had insisted upon it, despite Benton's protests, and she had even gone so far as to call Robyn herself – inviting her to come Saturday afternoon, picked up by Thalia in town after her massage, and thus guaranteed to arrive in time for a walk around the farm before dark and the commencement of eating and drinking. For this, Thalia had decided, there would be two other couples: a pair of graduate students called Stephan and Lilly Hartmann, who had been finishing their Ph.D. theses for close to a decade and acted as surrogate parents to young initiates like Thalia; and Milton and Elaine Totting – Milton was Malcolm's older brother and taught in the Biology Department, while Elaine had achieved a small reputation as a Vegetarian Psychic.

This guest list was invented by Thalia, who said that she didn't mind the idea of a dinner party, but she wasn't going to have a group of Benton's enemies over from the English Department just to impress Robyn Marler who was, after all, as well as being a single woman badly deserving company on a weekend so near to Christmas, also an American who, strictly speaking, should never have been offered a job at a Canadian university when there were probably hundreds of equally qualified Canadians getting a lot lonelier driving cabs or waiting in unemployment lines.

At the last moment, Saturday morning, Milton Totting telephoned to say that he and Elaine had both come down with the seasonal flu and would be unable, sorry, to come, much as he had been looking forward to meeting with the renowned Miss Marler of whom he had heard many wonderful things. Listening to Milton compose his long and pompous sentences, Benton wondered how the two Totting brothers could be related.

"For God's sake, don't tell Milton," Malcolm had said, his first words when they took off the oxygen mask. "It's an old Celtic custom that you shouldn't have to hire your own undertaker."

By Saturday afternoon at three o'clock, Benton had finished cleaning the house, had changed Jonah for the sixth time that day, and was trying to decide, as he had been for three hours, exactly what he should wear. He wanted a costume that was essentially formal, clothes which would announce to Robyn Marler that here was a man to be taken seriously, a man who wore a suit in his own home the way a

Spanish peasant wore a shirt and tie when he stepped out to trim the hedges; a man in possession of his life who *could not be dislodged without the gravest consequences.* At five minutes to three, in fact, he was wearing the dark-blue suit that he had not worn since his wedding, and was sitting downstairs with a very light drink, reading the most recent *Times Literary Supplement*, airmail edition, and keeping one eye on Jonah who, in an excess of splendid good behaviour, was sitting happily in the centre of the living room floor, his tiny little fingers laced together, enjoying the feeling of the sun shining on his face.

At that moment, Benton remembered that he had promised to take Robyn for a walk around the farm. In fact he had already planned numerous anecdotes to tell her that would, on the one hand, be amusing and therefore welcoming, so that she would feel he truly wanted her to be sharing his house for a few days, and on the other hand a little on the staid and humourless side, just like Milton Totting. This combination would allow her to see that, drinks in the afternoon aside, he really was a very boring fellow, certainly not worth the trouble of a brilliant and widely translated writer whose book was a surprise bestseller in Japan; it might even demonstrate what an extraordinarily dull and serious person he was, a complete zero in fact, redeemed only by his desperate existential commitment to the faulty but beautiful Thalia Stewart, a commitment that could not be breached for one second without both betraying a helpless young mother, and corrupting beyond repair what little was left of his own worthless moral fibre.

Unfortunately, Benton realized, racing up the stairs, all these noble purposes of costume were going to be wasted if he didn't change, not even a totally insufferable asshole would dress up in his wedding suit to take the golden whore of the heartland for a walk in the barnyard.

He had his suit pants off and his jeans half on when he heard the kitchen door open. Jonah shrieked and, pulling on his jeans, Benton rushed stocking-footed to rescue his son.

"Sorry," Milton Totting said, standing at the doorway to the living room. Benton reached for Jonah, whose happiness had been changed by Milton's arrival into total terror.

"It's all right," Benton said, stooping to swing Jonah into his arms. "Strangers make him nervous."

"We felt better and decided to come up for the afternoon, anyway. I tried to telephone but the line was busy."

"Party line," Benton said automatically, "the woman up the road is on the phone a lot these days. The other night her husband slipped and broke his leg."

"Elaine is out in the car," Milton said. "I just thought I would come in first to make sure you were ready to receive us."

"Bring her in, for God's sake, I was just – " Here Benton looked down at his shirt, his tie, his unzipped jeans.

Milton nodded and went out again. Benton, this time with Jonah under one arm, rushed upstairs to take off his tie and substitute the heavy cableknit sweater that Thalia had given him the first Christmas after they had met.

When he returned to the living room Milton and Elaine were standing and looking at his books. Elaine had a red nose, which Benton recognized as the nose she developed from crying during her fights with Milton, and Milton had a bruise under his right eye which Benton hadn't noticed before.

"Let's have a drink," Benton said into the silence.

Milton and Elaine both turned towards him at once.

"I don't know, old man," Milton began.

But Elaine cut him off and held out her hand.

Soon they were armed with three stiff scotches, and as the grey December sky filled with snow, Benton calculated his chances of getting the Tottings drunk and battling again before dark, so they would leave before the evening proper commenced.

"Have you heard from Malcolm?" Milton asked.

"A card or two," Benton said. "Oh, and there was a letter." This letter was his first lie of the afternoon. It was, he thought, in honour of Robyn – whom he was now eagerly awaiting, because she would surely soften the problem of these unwanted Tottings.

"I haven't heard at all," Milton said gloomily.

"He doesn't like to write Milton," Elaine added. "He confuses Milton with his father."

"I thought your father was dead."

"That's why he uses Milton. He's far too immature to stand on his own, and thank God he doesn't get himself fired by taking out his authority problems on the Dean. Really, he ought to give Milton a portion of his salary for keeping him stable."

Benton found that his scotch had disappeared and he went into the kitchen to get himself another. When he got back Elaine was sitting on the floor, beside Jonah.

"He *is* cute," Elaine said.

"He is," Benton agreed.

"It's too bad you didn't have children with Penny."

"Just as well now," Benton said. "It would have been hard on the children."

"Don't you think you would have stayed married?" Elaine looked around the room. Benton recognized the moment – she and Milton had come out to the farm often enough when he was married to Penny, and after the marriage broke up they had tried to console and patch up. Of course Benton hadn't told them about Thalia, but it wouldn't have mattered if he had. Milton considered graduate students to be expendable fodder intended for the amusement of the faculty – as long as they had paid their tuition.

"No," said Benton, "of course not." But he was distracted because he had seen, through the window, Thalia turning up the drive.

"I would never get divorced," Elaine said, as Benton headed once more out of the living room and into the kitchen, this time to start heating Jonah's formula.

Milton followed him into the kitchen and stood behind him while Benton put the bottle and the pot of water onto the stove to heat.

"We didn't know whether to come," said Milton in a low voice.

"It's nice to see you, and Thalia would have been so disappointed."

"Elaine hasn't been feeling herself lately. She's been thinking of changing doctors."

"You should take it easy on her," Benton said, turning around to see, behind Milton's surprised look, Robyn and Thalia stumbling in the door.

At the sight of Robyn, her arms around a brown paper bag of groceries, marching in confidently as if she were already mistress of this house, Benton's stomach pumped a vigorous dose of fear into his system, and he could feel the sweat spring out along his back.

"Take these," Thalia instructed, handing her own shopping to Benton. "I hope the red wine didn't get too cold. God, the massage almost killed me today. When he put his fingers into my spine I thought I was going to scream."

"You said he was a fairy."

"Now he says he wants to get interested in women."

"I want to go for a walk before it gets dark," Robyn announced.

"You take her," Thalia said. "I'll go put Jonah down."

Benton stood paralyzed, only his head moving as it nodded back and forth to listen to the commands of the two women. Perhaps, he thought, they might have already discussed him, his own particular will-less state, and settled his fate between them. That thought he found comforting: if only they could decide between them what was best, a solution that made *them* happy, then he was certain he would go along.

"Well, come on," Robyn said. "What are you waiting for?"

While Benton put on his boots and coat, he asked Milton and Elaine if they would like to tour the barns. "I don't know why you'd want to," he added. "They don't look any different than the last time."

"We should go home," Elaine said. Since telling Benton she would never get divorced she had been standing and chewing her lip in the kitchen doorway.

"Stay," Benton said. "I insist."

"We weren't going to come at all," Milton repeated, but by this time Benton had finished dressing and was pushing Robyn out the door in front of him, so that all he could do was turn and call back, "I'm glad you did, help yourself to another scotch before Thalia gets down."

Outside the sky was already starting to turn dark. Across the frozen snow the wind was blowing from the north, starting a quick ache in the earlobe where Benton had once gotten frostbite.

It was already too late to walk around the land. But instead of taking Robyn to the barn where the sheep and cows were, Benton led her to the chicken coop, a small, low-ceilinged building with a tiny row of windows facing south. He opened the door and made Robyn go ahead into the blackness. Then he followed her in, switching on the light. Instantly there was a bizarre glare of white: Benton had put a floor in the old coop and insulated the walls in styrofoam. His plan had been to finish, before winter, construction of a studio where Thalia, in a place where she couldn't be interrupted by Jonah, would finish her thesis.

"Nice," Robyn said.

"It's not done yet."

She turned to him. The room was small, smaller even than Benton's office at the university. He noticed that Robyn was wearing a thick fur coat, in which he would have liked to bury himself, and that her face seemed ten years younger.

"It's very nice just the same," Robyn said. "I really think so." She took a couple of steps, which brought her across the room.

"I meant to finish it sooner. I don't always get things done." The light came from a bare bulb hanging on two wires taped into the ceiling fixture. There were, along the walls, jagged rectangular holes cut for further outlets. Thalia liked to use an electric typewriter, and while he was doing the wiring Benton had tried to imagine different places where she might want to sit, ways she would position the light. The idea of Thalia out in this chicken coop that he had converted to a study for her thesis gave him pleasure. All the while he worked on it he held fast to the image of himself in the house, surrounded by the smell of the soups he was going to learn to cook, Jonah crawling on the living room carpet, while outside, Thalia – who after everything was said and done had surely not become pregnant with Jonah just to force him out of his marriage – finally picked up the thread of her life, the thread that Benton had broken the night Malcolm Totting tried to kill himself.

"You love Thalia very much," Robyn said. She was giving him her sad smile again.

"I guess I do," Benton said. "No, that sounds silly. I do love her. I *really* love her."

"I believe you."

"Well, I guess it *is* true then." He smiled. The room was cold, but not nearly so cold as outside, and it came into his mind that they could lie down on the insulated plywood floor and go to sleep under Robyn's thick fur coat.

"I loved my husband very much," Robyn said. "I was very sad when he died." She was wearing her sad smile almost permanently now, and she spoke her words very slowly and carefully, as if they were an emotional arithmetic at which Benton was a slow learner.

"I'm very sorry he died," Benton said.

"I don't think he went to heaven."

"No."

"I don't think he went anywhere."

"No." Benton realized that his face was wet. It really *was* too bad that Robyn Marler's husband had died. If she loved him. She had reached out for him and he had been taken away. "I'm sorry," Benton said.

"It's not your fault." Robyn smiled, only this time it was not her sad smile, but the flashy one that snapped like electric fingers.

"Well," Benton said, "people will be wondering where we are."

"We're here," Robyn said. "You've been telling me how much you love Thalia, how sorry you are that my husband died."

Benton looked down at his boots. The snow had melted into little black puddles. "Actually," he said, "I think it was you who was telling me." Saying the words made him feel sick to his stomach, the way he used to feel when he quarrelled with Penny.

"You'll forgive me," Robyn said. Not a statement, but not entirely a question. A hope. She had stepped forward and put her hand on his canvas parka. "Will you forgive me?"

If he kissed her, Benton knew, his world would end. The slender thread connecting him to Thalia, keeping him on this absurd farm from which he could see, hear, almost *smell* the city would snap, and he would be plunged into the river of Robyn Marler, her untrustworthy New York eyes and smile, the thundering vacuum of her too-successful soul.

And yet, Benton had to admit to himself, he was forty-three years old and he knew what it was like when a woman asked him to kiss her. This wasn't it. Robyn Marler, the much-translated Coleridgean who was also a defenseless and bereaved widow, was not closing her eyes and turning up her lips, she was not opening her eyes wide and sizzling his nerves, she was not pressing stray parts of herself against him and giving him hints that there was more to come. She was just asking him to forgive her for a somewhat nasty remark.

"Of course," Benton said, "there's nothing to forgive. Please." And then he stayed, without moving, while Robyn led the way out, ducking slightly at the low door.

Outside the sky had turned from dark to black. Mounted on a hydro pole was a light which illuminated the hard-packed snow paths between the house and the buildings. As he walked behind Robyn Marler, Benton breathed the cold air deep into his lungs, his heart fairly leaping with exultation. He had done it, truly *done* it; for the first time in his life he had looked into the eye of desire and had been able to turn around and walk away.

Benton opened the kitchen door for Robyn, feeling so much the master of the situation that he let his hand fall against her coat. She neither responded nor withdrew, only waited patiently while he fumbled with the latch. And then the door was open and he could hear Thalia's happy laughter from the living room; she was standing by the fireplace, a glass of wine in her hand, waving it towards her friends, the Hartmanns, who must have arrived while he was in the chicken coop with Robyn. And while Benton kicked off his boots and went to make new drinks for himself and Robyn, he could see the Tottings sitting sullenly on a sofa. The three young people had probably made them feel old and out-of-place, and Benton experienced a happy satisfaction at the thought that he, though older than Milton Totting, felt perfectly at ease with the younger generation.

When he entered the living room, the fireplace was roaring and spitting with the cedar he had split for it that morning. As he came up to her, Thalia passed a joint to him – no doubt courtesy of the Hartmanns – and after taking a demure puff he passed it on to Robyn, who sucked down the smoke with such greedy force that the fire split apart a seed and made it explode with a spark that tore open the paper and surprised Robyn into dropping it.

"Professor Marler!" Stephan exclaimed admiringly. He started another joint at which Robyn again took her turn. After it had made several rounds, Benton carried it over to the Tottings.

"Thank you, Benton, but not tonight," Milton said, as though it were a telephone conversation. "We really must go." Thalia had put on a record, one of her favourite raucous English bands who dyed their hair purple, and Benton could barely hear Milton's voice above the noise. "We just meant to drop in, you see, but I thought we'd wait until you came back to the house." This he said disapprovingly, as if he knew it was only a matter of time before he and Elaine, dropping in on a Sunday afternoon, would find Benton and Robyn cosily ensconced while poor Thalia and Jonah were buried out in the back field.

But before Benton could reply, Thalia was leaning over the Tottings, insisting that they absolutely *must* stay, that she would even change the music to suit them, and without waiting for a reply she sprang over to the record player and put on a suite of oboe sonatas.

Benton, whose head was swirling from what he realized must be close to half a bottle of scotch, as well as a number of healthy lungfuls of what Hartmann had whispered to be "real Cambodian shit," felt as though he had been suddenly hurled from the centre of the storm which he had just faced down, the decadent lust of the ravaged widow, into a deep and languid tropical swimming pool, an aqueous jungle of low moaning sounds. And yet, amazingly, Milton looked happy; a greasy purr was lighting up his face. Even Elaine was smiling and lighting a new cigarette while sipping primly at the ice water to which Milton must have confined her.

"You will stay," Benton said. His body broke in half as he leaned over them, plucking from Milton's diffident hand its empty glass of scotch; yes, good, the Tottings were staying, it was important that they stay because this was Thalia's event, Thalia's weekend. Somehow it must be a dazzling triumph, a riot of non-stop fun.

"That's right," Milton replied, "a riot of non-stop fun."

"I must have spoken aloud," Benton said.

"A dazzling triumph of reason," Milton said.

In his hand Benton held Milton's glass. He clamped his teeth around his tongue so that Milton could not hear him say how desperately, how deeply, how with incredible and total sincerity he wished that his best and only friend Malcolm were here in place of this leather-stuffed fart of a brother.

"You know, Benton," Milton leaned over, "I don't think that I've ever understood until this evening exactly why my brother values you so much. You have a thick skull, but beneath it you're such a fine person, a truly *fine* person."

"Fuck you," Benton said. His words were like bubbles and he hoped, hopelessly, that they would burst through the surface of the swimming pool.

"Fuck," Milton said. "A fine word. Benton, get me another fucking glass of scotch, will you?"

"Fuck you," Benton said, but this time he managed to get himself turned and aimed in the direction of the kitchen. Drunk, it was amazing, the scotch had absolutely gone to his head. It seemed now like years since he had been on the wagon, years since he had been properly drunk, so long ago that he must have been a different person then, a carefree married man who went alone to the occasional party at his best friend's apartment and got drunk and sang old Beatles songs and stayed up half the night until settling into some innocent infidelity on the couch that was there for exactly that purpose. And even in the morning after those drunks, he never felt remorse, guilt, fear of getting caught; he would wake up ready to roar, wake up with the fire blazing in him, and rush into Malcolm's kitchen to stoke himself with coffee for the exhilarating day.

Drink, fire, air: in those days he had been like an eagle;

now he was stuck on the farm, rooted as Thalia called it, living on the land – yes, he was on the land all right, he had been squashed to the fucking ground until he could feel the earth grinding up through the yellowing soles of his feet. Earth and water, he was diving down with age, this new drunk was the drunk of the second half of his life. Under the horizon where the sun would never rise, where his heart was filled with earth and water. "You know what," he whispered to Thalia; he was in the kitchen now and had walked up to her despite the fact that she was leaning back against the sink, eyes closed, happily letting Stephan Hartmann put his arm around her, "I feel like a vegetarian tonight."

Thalia opened her eyes – he had forgotten what a fierce green they could be – and stepped into him, away from Stephan's shadow, her arms now around his own neck the way she used to kiss him. "Benton, we're having *stew* tonight." And then, giggling as she pushed him back, all the way across the kitchen from the sink to the refrigerator, pressing herself against him and biting his ear, she whispered, "Benton, you're so drunk; Benton, you're not mad at me?"

"I love you, stupid."

"I love you."

She kissed him and he held her tight, wrapping his arms around the slender back of this beautiful stranger while she bit his ear and made little knives of desire shoot through his fingers.

Then suddenly she whirled away, skimming across the kitchen like a skinny dancing heron, bowing not to Stephan but to Lilly, who was holding out her pudgy arms to her. And as Thalia rushed into Lilly's embrace Benton turned to Stephan, to exchange a shrug, but Stephan was laughing so hard that his eyes were squinted into tiny blind sparks.

"You're all drunk," Benton said, but quietly, sad to see that they were all still birds while he was reduced to burrowing through the earth; and feeling suddenly teary and self-pitying he poured Milton half a glass of scotch. If Milton had one gene in common with his sorely-missed brother, surely this would set it free. And then, opening the freezer to get the ice cubes he scraped his knuckles, and when he turned to ask Thalia to kiss them better she was already behind him, her stealthy hands sneaking up his sweater to scare him. He shrieked in loud delight.

"Are you all right?"

"Fine, really fine."

"You're sure?" But just as her repeated question made him unsure, her hands squeezed him again and the knives of desire came back, he was a bird with them after all.

When Benton got back to the living room Elaine had changed the music again, back to the raucous British, and had thrown off her shoes to dance with Stephan, who was smoking another joint. She had unwound her black hair from the bun she always wore. It swung around her shoulders like a witch's mop as she danced, except that she wasn't really dancing, she was just kicking her heels up into the air and waving her arms around like a crazy woman, singing along to the music while Stephan passed her the joint and laughed in encouragement.

"Some party," Milton said.

For some reason this made Benton realize that it had been ages since he had seen Robyn. He turned his head around the room so quickly that he staggered. As he fell towards the floor he kept twisting, and as he did he saw Robyn coming down the stairs, smiling and quite at ease as if she had come from her own room – which, of course, she had since she was staying for the weekend – and then Benton heard the doctor's voice telling him that it wasn't good for diabetics to get drunk, and he saw an image of a graph, his blood-sugar going up and down like a rollercoaster, up and down to one knee with his leg twisted beneath him – there was a moment when he felt himself beginning to black out the way he had that first night with Thalia – but the moment became a loud popping sound, it was the sound of his own clarity bursting through the surface of the swimming pool, and he could feel his eyes jumping open with the pressure, his ears hurting, and in a completely controlled sequence to his fall he began to unwind himself, amazing himself as he gradually got to his feet, grinning at Robyn whose eyes had never left his, whose large and violet eyes were the depths through which he had been swimming, whose eyes now watched him in that same detached and sad way he had first seen in his office, and smiling first at her and then at Milton, Benton rubbed his leg and said, "Sorry, I must have twisted my ankle, sometimes it goes like that."

"You didn't spill a drop." Milton Totting's pompous voice declared this with such approval that Benton realized that his wish had come true: Milton wasn't such a bad fellow after all. Beneath that swollen grease was a person worth having to dinner.

"No," Robyn said, "he didn't spill a drop."

Now she was standing close to him, much closer than she had in the shed, and her eyes, he hadn't been mistaken when he saw her from his fallen position, were truly burning; she, too, was drunk, stoned, the golden whore of the heartland was on the rampage and Benton could see her passion exploding like violet ribbons from her eyes.

"You really are amazing," Robyn said. She was wearing a silk dress of dark scarlet that was tied modestly at the neck and at the wrists, and she put one of her hands on his arm. For this occasion all the nicotine had been scrubbed away, but Benton was still aware of the used, hide-like skin that had been leathered by empire and corruption, by the same decades he himself had travelled through, by losing to life first, and then to death.

"You think too much," Robyn said. She had dropped her voice into a private murmur meant for him alone.

"I believe in thinking."

"I don't," Robyn said. And she looked to Milton and in the same tone asked: "Do you?"

"No," he said, then looked over at his wife. His bruised eye had taken on a dark and pleasantly shiny hue.

"There you go," Robyn said. "I told you you were amazing and I was right."

In the middle of the night, Benton woke up. One minute he had been asleep and the next he was lying on his back, body rigid, eyes staring at the ceiling. He breathed deeply, felt his muscles relax. The fear was in his stomach, a nauseous feeling that wanted to be thrown up. He reached his arm out, turned very carefully to see who he would find lying beside him. But it was only Thalia, her breathing deep and regular. He shifted slightly in the bed to discover if she was naked. She was, good: when she was angry with him she wore a nightgown to bed.

Benton, feeling better, sat up and reached for a cigarette. Once he had quit smoking for six years. When he would wake up, drenched with sweat, the fear was that he had given in and smoked a cigarette.

Through the window he could see bright patterns of stars. That meant, he knew, that it would be very cold outside. As the thought entered his mind, like a switch, the furnace went on. For a few seconds the house shook like a ship in a storm. But instead of instructing himself to go to the hardware store, Benton now calculated that almost half the heating season was over. During the Christmas holidays he would call a repairman to clean the motor and fix the faulty hinge.

His gaze fixed on the shining metal roof of the chicken coop. He could remember, with perfect clarity, going out to show it to Robyn. Sentences had been exchanged: he couldn't remember the words, but the sequence of feelings came back – somehow, as he was doing the exact right thing, the proper thing that he had decided, he had nevertheless slid into her embrace.

Benton spat out a long spiral of smoke. Along with everything else, the fine, stoned feeling he'd had was coming back. He felt good. Alive. He had survived some terrible temptation, a temptation even more difficult than not smoking a cigarette, and now the sky was so proud of him that soon it would break apart – the way it used to fifteen years ago – and show him another day. He got up out of bed and put on his housecoat. At this moment, stretching it across his broad shoulders, he almost wished he had succumbed, had fallen to the charms of the great golden whore, taken America itself in his arms so that he could, in his drunkenness, have mixed his own corruption with her yellowed skin, taken her in his arms and then risen up out of them, like right now, risen before the dawn and driven back to his faithful, waiting Thalia.

He stepped out of the bedroom and walked downstairs. His feet knew the way in the dark and soon he was in the kitchen, brewing up a cup of coffee the way he used to. The coffee was like a hot slap against his tongue. It poured down his throat and fired up his belly. The kitchen was a mess of heaped plates and dirty pots. He took a swallow from an open bottle of wine, spat it into the sink, then carried his coffee into the living room.

Now he remembered the second trip out to the chicken coop – for a moment he panicked with the memory, afraid that he had lost his hold after all. Then the picture came back: after he and Thalia had seen the Tottings to their car, he had insisted on showing Thalia exactly how he intended to fix the chicken coop as her studio.

They had stumbled inside, but he didn't switch on the light. He just closed the door behind him and threw his arms around her, desperately wanting to beg her forgiveness. But of course there was nothing to be forgiven for; he didn't dare explain that he had almost kissed Robyn Marler.

Thalia, drunk, wanted to make love on the floor, had even wrestled him to the cold plywood. But he had been too dizzy, so they just sat silently in the dark, their backs squeaking against the styrofoam, looking out at the sky.

"I don't care," Thalia whispered fiercely. "I feel so close to you tonight."

Then they went back to the house. Robyn had gone up to bed in their absence and the Hartmanns, suddenly lucid and sober, were carrying dirty glasses and ashtrays into the kitchen. "Don't," Thalia protested, but they had insisted on at least cleaning the living room; and now, sitting in his favourite chair, beside the bookcases he had made, Benton felt that certain grim sense he had sometimes at Malcolm's house, the last one awake, the mourner sitting in the party's morgue, remembering the triumphs and disasters, trying to add up the score so that it came out in his favour.

It was all right, Benton said to himself. It *was*. Every time his mind went back to the moment he had sat on the floor with Thalia he felt tired and listless. But when he remembered the time with Robyn, a raw nerve pulsed. He *had* managed to resist her. He had turned her down, even if she had been the one to apologize, and she would never forgive him. So he would never have to turn her down again.

Benton stood up. He had never been so drunk in his own house. Suddenly he felt overwhelmingly exhausted. Every step was painful, his muscles felt bruised from the inside. He walked slowly to the kitchen, turned out the light, then started up the stairs.

At the bathroom he pushed open the door to brush his teeth. Even as the door began to move, he realized that the light was on. He hated to waste electricity. As that thought was forming, the smell of steam and perfume swept it away, but he didn't have the presence of mind, despite what Robyn had said about his compulsive thinking, to actually do anything but continue to open the door, thoughtlessly following one strange clue after another like a dog who will run a trail until he bashes his brains into a tree. And then the door was open and he saw Robyn Marler, standing stark naked on the rug beside his bathtub.

"Excuse me," Robyn said, "I didn't think to bring my housecoat."

"It's all right."

Robyn then stepped, as she had been about to, into the bathtub, and as Benton watched, slid down into the water until she was lying, full length, on her back.

The party had washed away the lines on her face, her body was slender and perfectly formed – she might have been Thalia's smaller twin. Her skin was a smooth and dazzling ivory, with a young, glossy sheen as though it had been made from the whites of rare eggs.

"Well," Robyn said.

"Well," Benton repeated. All the fearfulness that had attacked him the past two months was now gathered together and raging in his nerves. Even his own choked breath sounded like Thalia, rushing in to discover this lurid scene.

"Well," Robyn said. "I feel like a character in an Italian movie."

"I was just on my way to brush my teeth," Benton said.

"That's a good idea," Robyn said. "Why don't you brush your teeth?" Her breasts were bobbing on the water like small pear-shaped lifeboats.

Benton took his toothbrush from the rack. It was a bright-blue plastic with white nylon bristles. He covered them carefully with toothpaste, all the while looking away from Robyn, then bent over the sink. In the mirror he saw Robyn staring at him.

"I'm sorry about this afternoon," Robyn said.

"Don't – "

"Sometimes I get lonely for a man."

Benton lifted the toothbrush towards his mouth. Robyn shifted in the bath, sending tiny whorls of water from her nipples.

"Many men must find you – "

"Not so many," Robyn said.

"I do," Benton said. He turned and, still holding his toothbrush, walked out of the bathroom, closing the door carefully behind him, and continued down the hall to the bedroom. Thalia was lying awake in bed, the lamp on, reading.

"What's everyone doing?"

"I made some coffee," Benton said. "Robyn's taking a bath. I walked in on her by mistake."

"I hope Jonah doesn't wake up."

Benton took off his housecoat, put his toothbrush in its pocket, and lay down beside Thalia, pulling the covers over himself. Thalia switched off the lamp and curled beside him. Benton, on his back, was conscious that he was staring at the same spot on the ceiling that he had looked at when he woke up. He also wished that he hadn't woken up. Thalia, putting one leg across his thighs, rested her head on his chest.

"Do you mind?" Thalia asked sleepily.

"No." In the dark he could hear the furnace starting to shudder again, his own heart skipping with it, struggling to break free.

Winter light splintered from the white snow, from the plate glass windows of the offices banked next to his own, from the white scrubbed stone of the university buildings. Long brilliant shards pierced his office, threw themselves against his own white-painted walls, lay like shining spears across the photograph of the American writer.

One of these days, Benton thought, one of these days soon, he himself was going to break apart under the force of all this harsh and glaring energy. But for now he was alive, safe and still.

He was sitting in his office, his pre-Christmas appointments with students finally finished, and he was looking at the picture of F. Scott Fitzgerald. It was a signed photograph. Benton had found it in a second-hand bookstore in Paris when he was researching the book. In it, Fitzgerald was still young and full of juice, the wide-set eyes hungrily staring out at the world, eager to swallow and record, to render the vision in prose as clear as a dream, as sparkling as champagne, as hopeful as the hopeful mornings he must have had waking with Zelda, heart popping open with love.

Remembering the prose of Fitzgerald, the shock of reading each perfect line, Benton stood up in surprise. Twenty years ago, when he had been seized by the dream of words, the perfect surface of Fitzgerald's language, he had wanted to write not a biography but a novel of his own. In those days, too, he had been living in Toronto.

When Robyn came into his office Benton was looking out the window to the snow. He turned around, and even before her name came into his mind he saw that her hair had been cut to shoulder length.

"What happened?"

"Am I early?"

"Your hair."

"Oh, that. Do you like it? I've wanted to cut it for years but Hugh always insisted he would leave me if I did. Today is the second anniversary of his death and I thought, instead of crying all day, that I would go to the hairdresser. How do you like it?"

She stopped suddenly, searched in her purse for a cigarette. She had never before mentioned her husband by name and Benton found himself stepping towards her, as though she would have to be consoled.

"Stephan was the one who talked me into it," Robyn said.

"Stephan?" Benton repeated. Despite himself he felt a flare of jealousy.

"When I told him about Hugh's loving my long hair Stephan said that I was being like a primitive widow, throwing herself on her husband's funeral pyre."

"When did he tell you this?" Benton said stupidly, hating himself as he heard the words.

"At lunch," Robyn said, "the other day. He wanted me to read the first chapters of his thesis."

"A brilliant student," Benton said. "Quite exceptional." He sat down. Robyn's face, which used to be half-hidden by the tidal waves of her long hair, now looked pretty, younger, more vulnerable. The colouring, too, had been renewed, so that the sharp light from the window was muted and golden in the wisps of hair that curled about her shoulders.

"I admire Jews that way," Robyn said. "They always have such a sinister twist of mind."

Benton felt a blush starting, the way it had the day Robyn had pretended to be having an affair with a student, and he wondered if once again she was saying something to test him. But even as he expected her to laugh and apologize her mouth moved into that sudden flash of a smile, like a fencer flicking his sword to see if the tip had drawn blood.

"What are you doing this afternoon?"

"I was going to do my Christmas shopping today," Benton said. "I left my car to get repaired. It's not going to be ready until this evening."

"Let me come with you. I always feel so stupid buying presents. You can encourage me to be extravagant." Again she smiled, but this time it was the sad-wise smile she had shown him a week ago in the chicken coop, the smile he had imagined on her face as he turned his back on her in the bathroom. The following morning it had been Thalia, at the breakfast table, who brought up the incident.

"Benton tells me that he interrupted your bath."

"I always like company in the bathroom," Robyn had said. "He could at least have brought me a drink."

"It's silly how easily men can be embarrassed," Thalia had continued. "Nothing is more natural than being naked."

Now Benton stood up. "We'll go shopping," he said. "Then we can have a drink before it's time for me to pick up my car."

"I don't want to waste your whole afternoon," Robyn said hesitantly.

But as she spoke Benton felt as though one of the blades of light had slipped between his ribs. He stopped, suppressing a gasp, reached one hand out to the bookshelf to steady himself. He was in love with Robyn Marler. How could he not have known? Since the day he had met her he had been happy only in her presence, had thought of nothing and no one but her, had centred his daily existence on their apparently chance and casual meetings.

"What's wrong?"

"Nothing," Benton said. He straightened up. The physical pain was gone but the calm white light of the room was now a swirling rainbow of turbulent colours. *I've had a heart attack*, he thought to himself, *an attack of the heart*.

"Are you feeling sick?"

"Not at all, no. It's just that I've been sitting in my chair all afternoon. I'm getting to be an old man, dizzy every time I make a sudden move."

"Don't make any sudden moves," Robyn said. She was standing very close to him, her arm linked through his to support him. Looking down to her face Benton saw the violet eyes of Robyn Marler turning slowly upwards, opening wider as if to grasp exactly what was happening.

"I'm all right," Benton said. "Let's get outside, into the air."

A few minutes later they were walking across the snow-covered common of the campus. The afternoon sun that had been so dazzling only a few minutes before was now masked by thin yellow-white clouds, and though the sky was mostly clear, there was falling – from somewhere – thin needles of snow. The wind gusted it into eddies, whipped it like sand across their faces.

Soon they were at the subway entrance. And by the time they were riding up the escalators of the Eaton Centre, Benton felt that he could breathe again, that the scene in his office was safely behind him, stored away with other scenes with Robyn, other embarrassing incidents from other moments in his life.

Through his body he felt a warm and buzzing hum, as if his blood had turned to sweet honey: the feeling of love released. When Robyn turned to ask his advice about a blouse for her sister, her voice rang through him like a low bell. And when he bought a sweater for Thalia he held it in his hands and squeezed the soft wool between his fingers as though it was Robyn he had in his hands, Robyn's skin he was wanting to warm, Robyn's pleasure he was hoping to excite.

Passing through the crowd they were sometimes squeezed together, sometimes separated by other bodies. The warm press of Robyn's shoulder and breast, her sudden absence, became the rhythm of Benton's breathing. Once she stopped to look in a window and Benton, wandering in his daze, was almost a hundred feet away before he realized that the rhythm was broken and she was out of his sight.

By the time they were finished shopping it was six o'clock. "It's time for me to go now," Benton said.

They were in the middle of the shopping mall, surrounded by a crowd so thick that they were now permanently pressed together. Benton, trying to step away, felt suddenly as he had that night on his farm. He was looking desire in the eye, and he was walking away from it.

"Goodbye," Robyn said.

When Benton got to the garage they told him that they had been trying to phone him at his office. Something to do with the carburetor, a missing part that would take an extra day.

"I need the car," Benton said. "You should have told me it might take longer."

"You can have mine," the manager said, "if it's that bad."

"No. It's not that bad."

He left the garage and walked down the street to a hotel where he and Malcolm had often gone to drink when they were graduate students. But when he went into the bar, Benton saw that the old wooden tables and chairs had been replaced by stuffed armchairs and sofas: the place looked like a gigantic living room. In it, laughing and talking, were crowds of happy drinkers, and the sounds of Christmas toasts and singing rolled towards him like a thick fog.

In the lobby he found a telephone.

"I can sleep at my office," Benton said. "They promised the car would be ready at noon."

"Don't sleep at your office, your back will be sore for a week."

Benton, silent, heard noises in the background. "Who's there?"

"Stephan and Lilly. They came out to bring us a bottle of wine. Too bad you didn't know about the car earlier, you could have driven with them."

"I could stay at a hotel," Benton said.

"Stay at Robyn's. You should know your way around the couch well enough. And you could take her out to dinner. She must be lonely."

"She doesn't seem lonely."

"I love you, Benton."

"I love you."

"Don't make yourself miserable tonight. I'm sorry about the stupid car."

"I am, too."

Now Benton heard the explosive sound of Stephan's laugh. He started to reach for a cigarette, stopped himself, wished Malcolm were back from Paris so he could tell him how at forty-three he was a stupid adolescent again.

"I miss you, Benton."

"I miss you, too."

"I wish you were here, right now." Benton, thinking that Stephan Hartmann was hearing this soft and seductive voice, turned uncomfortably in the phone booth. In the hotel lobby he could see a drunken couple. The man was wearing a camel-hair coat, open to reveal a dazzling white shirt, an expensive-looking tie. The woman was leaning against him, smiling as though for an advertisement. Her teeth were white and gleaming, her eyes shone adoringly, but most spectacular of all was the dark fur she wore: sleek and oiled it glowed with life, as though it still belonged to some incredibly powerful and vital beast.

"Don't worry about me," Thalia said. "I'm fine here. Have a good time at dinner."

"Sit down," Robyn said. "Or stand if you prefer."

Benton, the door of Malcolm Totting's apartment already firmly closed behind him, kicked the snow from his galoshes. Then his cold fingers struggled with the buckles – the old-fashioned kind that Thalia had looked at with awe, as though he were wearing a Chippendale – before stepping into the living room.

"I keep forgetting," Robyn called from the kitchen, "that this was your friend's apartment. In fact, Malcolm Totting left me a note saying that if there was anything I couldn't work I should get in touch with you. It was actually a very charming note. I wish I'd saved it."

"Malcolm is famous for his notes."

Benton stood for a moment in the centre of the living room. His eye had been drawn to the corner where, unexpectedly, Robyn had placed a small, waist-high spruce tree. Around it was spiralled a long silver chain, and at its foot, surrounding the ceramic pot, were heaped dozens of Christmas cards – some open for display, others still in their envelopes.

Now Robyn emerged from the kitchen. "I made your

scotch with ice, but without water. I can't get used to Toronto's water – it doesn't taste poisonous enough."

They sat down, facing each other over Totting's coffee table.

"Your health," Robyn said.

"Merry Christmas."

Benton leaned back, lit a cigarette.

"You scared me this afternoon in your office, I have to admit. A friend of mine once had a heart attack that way. He was over for dinner, Hugh had gotten him awfully drunk, and when he stood up from the table he just swayed for a moment, clutched his chest, then fell to the floor. At first we thought he was joking. 'Just like Lawrence,' Hugh chortled. But then it turned out he'd had a serious attack."

Benton, staring at Robyn and feeling the blade between his own ribs again, slowly lowered his glass.

"He didn't die," Robyn said. "Not that night. But a couple of years later . . ."

She stopped; and Benton saw her eyes turning towards him once more, opening wider as they had during the afternoon, trying to comprehend what was happening to him. Again the colours of the room broke apart. He rubbed his eyes, but it was as if he were wearing those trick prism glasses he'd once had; nothing wanted to stay in its place. Benton picked up his glass again, tilted it back, and drained it. The whiskey was sour against his tongue and throat. He stubbed out his cigarette, started a new one. The doctor had warned him against smoking and drinking and, before he'd met Robyn, he'd almost stopped. It was, he now realized, since the fall that he'd begun drinking so heavily again. And he had virtually given up walking, too. The daily five miles had become a quick, weekly turn around the farm.

"It must be wonderful to have a young child."

"It is," Benton said. "Things happen, you never expect them." After Jonah had been born, Thalia, thin and too narrow in the hips, had bled profusely for a week. Like a white flower bleeding whiter, Benton had thought, vowing to protect her from anything bad that might ever happen to her, especially himself.

"You have a nice home, you and Thalia, a nice family."

"I know."

"Are you afraid of losing it?"

Benton looked at Robyn, whose violet eyes were now huge and round, staring into his once again.

"*Are* you afraid?"

"Yes."

"Don't be afraid, Benton. You don't have to be afraid of me."

"I'm not afraid of you, Robyn, I'm afraid of myself." As he said these words he felt the room jerk into focus. It was like the night in the chicken coop, the night Robyn had started to teach him this simple emotional arithmetic that seemed to be her specialty. One is one. One and one are two. Two minus one is one again.

"I wanted to be friends with you, Benton. I didn't want to hurt you."

"You haven't hurt me."

"I'm in love with you, Benton."

"No." Even as he said it, the word surprised him. It choked out of his throat, of its own volition, then seemed to lie between them, an unwanted stone. "I mean," Benton said, but he didn't continue. What he had started to say was that what he feared was not her love for him, but his love for her. But to say it would make it true, would make him responsible for the consequences. "Keep your thoughts to yourself, when it comes to romance. Then, when they pass, you can mourn for them alone." This had been Malcolm Totting's advice. Two years older than Benton, Malcolm had crossed the line of his fortieth birthday at a dead crawl, flayed by every crisis in the book: broken marriage, faltering health, professional insecurity, sexual hot flashes. By the time his sabbatical arrived he had barely the energy to get to

Paris. Privately, Benton suspected that Totting was going to Paris not to renew his French, eat wonderful food, do research, or get drunk at cut-rate prices – but to contemplate the romance of his failed suicide.

"What do you mean?"

Benton tried to imagine Thalia out at the farm. In Stephan's arms. In Lilly's arms. In the arms of Stephan and Lilly together.

"I mean," Benton said, "that I am in love with you, too." He looked across at Robyn and tried to smile. "I feel like such an idiot. Why are we sitting here saying that we love each other? Can't we eat dinner or something?"

"Let me make you an omelette, Benton. Eggs satisfy the nerves."

Benton stood up. For the third time in the past few months he felt himself beginning to blush. This time it caught him entire. He could feel his feet heating up, the gaps between his toes filling with sweat, the rush of hot blood turning his legs into pillars of fire, the invasion of his groin, a hot and itching sensation spreading across his belly. And at the same time he saw his hands had turned beet red, his ears were burning, even his lips seemed swollen and unable to move.

"Benton – "

"No – "

And then he had her in his arms, was squeezing her fiercely against him, crushing her into his chest so that he could feel her own heat joining to his.

"It took me a long time to get you here," Robyn whispered, when they were finally at the door to the bedroom.

I've been here before, Benton couldn't help thinking. But he said nothing. Instead he stared at the bed as though the blades twisting at his ribs could open his eyes, too, make them see beneath the antique quilt with which Robyn had covered the bed to the imprints of the bodies that had already lain there.

Then he turned to Robyn. In the broken light of his love, her face was like an icon's, dangerous and sharp.

"I can't do it," Benton groaned.

"Can't do what?"

"I can't leave Thalia for you. I'm too old, too tired, too – "

"Benton, Benton. You must think I'm such a bitch."

"What are we going to do?"

"Live our lives, Benton, as friends, lovers, never hurt each other. Promise?"

He had taken a room for himself at the hotel, explaining carefully to the bored clerk that because his car had broken down he had no luggage but the single Christmas present he had bought for his wife during the snowstorm. When he got to the room his hand trembled as he tried to insert the key. The key dropped to the carpet and, bending over, Benton wondered how he had reached that point of nervous exhaustion where he was afraid to rent a hotel room without making excuses.

The first thing he did was to take a bath. Soaking in the hot water he reminded himself of other irregular episodes that had been followed by this same cure, as if the poisons of alcohol and illicit sex could be removed only by direct skin contact with soap: a pore by pore cleansing guaranteed to wash away hangovers of every variety. When the telephone rang he was in the midst of rinsing his hair. But he leapt to answer it, grabbing a towel on his way. A man's voice, thick and stumbling with Christmas spirit, asked for Helen. Benton cut the voice off, saw that despite everything that had happened it was only midnight, and dialled his own home number.

He was about to hang up when Thalia answered on the sixth ring.

"Benton," he said. "I mean, it's me."

"Hello, you."

"Are they still there?" Benton felt so jealous that he began to shiver.

"Just going to sleep. Where are you?"

"At the hotel."

"I miss you," Thalia said.

"I miss you." Benton pulled the towel more tightly around his waist.

"Did you have dinner with Robyn?"

"Yes."

"Benton, is anything wrong?"

Thalia's voice was suddenly awake now, alert. Benton was reminded of the times when, still married, he used to wait until his wife was asleep and then creep downstairs to telephone Thalia. That was after she had told him she was pregnant, during the month-long interregnum between her announcement and his actual final separation. Those phone calls had been like secret dreams; long, whispered conversations during which Benton listened with one ear to Thalia's sleepy loving voice while the other wavered like an antenna to catch the first suspicious creak on the stairs. "You can't fight women," Malcolm Totting had told him repeatedly. "Women are professionals at love." "Love, yes," Benton once replied, "but men know how to betray." "Don't overreach yourself on that," Totting had advised.

"Benton? Are you there?"

"I'm here," Benton said. "Sorry, there *is* something wrong." He paused and for a brief moment he actually believed that he was going to blurt it out like a schoolboy, pass the burden to the ever-accommodating Thalia who, left on her own, might find other ways to amuse herself. "I feel terrible," Benton said. "You know how I hate hotels."

"Poor Benton. Have you been drinking?"

"The usual."

"You were going to stop drinking, doctor's orders."

"I still am," Benton said. "After Christmas, I promise. Nothing but mineral water and tomato juice."

"I wish you were here," Thalia said. Her voice was fully

awake and Benton realized that a wall of sorts had already grown up between them – a glass wall, perhaps, that was not even visible in the full light of love, but a wall, nonetheless, one that they would have to scale each time they wanted to be close, make love, trust.

"I'll come first thing in the morning, as soon as the car is ready."

"Love you," Thalia said, suddenly absent. But Benton, his own suspicions alerted, thought he could hear whispers behind her. Perhaps it was Hartmann going to the refrigerator, or even making faces to tease poor Thalia about having to talk to the staid and aging lover who had snatched her from the midst of youth and placed her, alone, in the middle of nowhere while he stumbled around downtown Toronto having his mid-life crisis.

"Benton, are you sure you're all right?"

"I'm tired," Benton said. "Let's spend tomorrow in bed, the way we used to."

As he hung up Benton realized that the bar would still be open, so he dressed again and went downstairs. In the elevator he decided that right after New Year's he would cut out everything but beer and the occasional glass of wine. Reassured by this resolve he ordered coffee and a double brandy: the coffee to snap him out of his depression, the brandy to put him to sleep.

By the time he went to bed he was, in fact, drunk; unpleasantly so. Three double brandies buzzed angrily through him, an unwanted extra skin between himself and the starched sheets.

Twice he picked up the telephone to dial Robyn's number; the third time he let it ring twice before he hung up. Then he turned on his stomach, bit into the pillow to keep his thoughts from forming, and fell into a deep sleep full of half-seen dreams and warnings.

"The greatest tragedy is a life unlived," Stephan Hartmann

said, and in his mouth the words took on such irony that they seemed to float at a miserable half-mast, barely hovering above the coffee table in Robyn Marler's living room. Benton, caught framed in the kitchen doorway, stopped and almost turned. For two hours Hartmann had been compulsively ranting to Robyn. First about his thesis, then on various subjects of departmental gossip. His hands couldn't stop moving, and under his thatch of black hair his face was red with enthusiasm. He had arrived at the apartment without calling in advance and when Robyn had answered the door he'd barged right through, nodding at Benton as if to acknowledge not only Benton's unexplained presence on a Wednesday afternoon but the whole new changed order of things. *He's been taking drugs*, had been Benton's first thought; but now Hartmann seemed under the influence of only a very boring type of pep pill.

From the refrigerator Benton took a beer for himself, a tin of apple juice for Robyn. Hartmann was already on his fourth cup of coffee.

It was late January, almost exactly a month since the afternoon he had gone Christmas shopping with Robyn; but so much had changed in that month he could hardly recognize himself. In the mornings when he dressed, his back often to Thalia, he was surprised to find his body fitting into the same old clothes. Even Jonah seemed not to have noticed that Benton's insides had been mysteriously rearranged: he still hugged Benton with abandon, clung to him in the middle of the night when he woke up with bad dreams, smiled at him with foolish happiness when he suddenly appeared from around some unexpected corner.

A month ago, Benton remembered, as he poured Robyn's apple juice into a glass, he had promised himself to stop drinking at New Year's. But now liquor was the least of his problems, merely one of the many lubricants he used to get himself through the various sticky patches of his day.

When Benton came into the living room Hartmann suddenly turned to him and said, as if he had been waiting all afternoon to deliver this essential line: "You are a good man. You *were* bad, like the rest of us, but now you are good. That's why it hurts."

"It doesn't hurt," Benton said, putting the glass of apple juice on the coffee table in front of Robyn. He stood above Hartmann, his palm protectively cupped around his beer bottle.

"I understand," Hartmann said. "You don't have to explain anything to me."

Benton sat down. Hartmann's eyes were trained on him like the open mouths of weapons. "It's your life," Hartmann said. "I understand completely."

Sentences crowded to Benton's tongue, but he didn't want to fend Hartmann off with a sharp reply; he wanted instead to lose himself in a sudden explosion of force, to meet the challenge of Hartmann's phoney stare with a slap that would send Hartmann flying across the room, out the door, out of his sight forever.

It was Robyn who finally broke the silence. She had picked up Hartmann's hand and patted it consolingly. When she let it go Hartmann made a fist, like a child about to have a tantrum. "It's time to go now, Stephan."

Hartmann jerked to his feet, his coffee unfinished, a cigarette still burning in the ashtray. "Benton," he said, "you can't just–" And then Benton knew that Thalia had sent him, after all, that there were no more mysteries: just Thalia at the farmhouse, listening to the furnace shudder, looking out at the snow, crying into the telephone. "What are you going to do?" Hartmann asked.

Robyn leaned forward to stub out Hartmann's cigarette. A button had come loose, and her dark shirt opened onto her smooth white skin, skin that felt as smooth and deep as it had first looked that night in the bathtub, and because they had gotten dressed so hastily when Hartmann came to the door she was wearing nothing under the shirt. Almost her entire breast was exposed, like a lost animal suddenly surfacing in a place it didn't belong. Benton, his mouth open to reply to Hartmann, found his attention caught by this unexpected intruder: *help me*, it seemed to say.

Hartmann's eyes were swinging back and forth from Benton to Robyn. The silence had prolonged itself so long that Benton found it quite natural to lift the bottle of beer to his mouth, take a swallow, set the bottle down, and then reach into his pocket for his cigarettes.

"What am I going to do?" Benton said, blowing smoke into the little triangle that their faces made. And finally looked at Hartmann, let his own eyes settle into Hartmann's the way a teacher finally seizes hold of his class. "For God's sake, Hartmann, you are surely the last person in the world who has the right to demand an explanation."

But even as Hartmann was going out the door, Benton wondered what sense his words could possibly make, even seem to make. Was he implying that Hartmann had slept with Thalia? With Robyn?

"I can't hurt Thalia," Benton said. He put out his old cigarette, lit a new one. It was essential to have the entire possibility stretching out in front of him. He walked to the window of the apartment hoping to see Stephan fade reassuringly from sight, but of course the street was too far away, only tiny cars crawling along and ant-like figures twisting amongst each other on the sidewalk.

The light in the room was breaking apart again, the way it always did these days. It made Robyn's golden hair shine brighter.

"I can't afford to love," Benton said.

Robyn stepped towards him. It was up to her, he thought. Things had gone too far. They were out of his hands. He had known it the night in the chicken coop, when he had tried to do his duty, like a man. Now it was up to the women: they could divide him up in whatever way was most convenient, following the lines of theory or love, it was really their decision.

"You look tired," Robyn said. She lifted her hand. Her palm slid underneath his shirt. Her fingers felt warm and alive against his bare chest. "Benton," she said. He had a sudden vision of them underneath a sheet, swimming in a tent of darkness, her body like a cool sea washing over him.

Totting came back early. Benton drove to the airport to pick him up. It was snowing heavily, and they had to plough the runways to keep them clear. By the time Totting's plane was allowed to land it was after midnight, and Benton, sitting on a moulded plastic seat in the Arrivals lounge, felt stunned with fatigue.

Totting emerged from Customs carrying only one suitcase. He was having the rest shipped in a trunk, he said. After only a few months away he seemed a different person: hair that had been greying was now almost entirely silver, he was thinner, and wore more expensive clothes.

"I felt better," Totting said. "I decided to come home before I got depressed again."

The highways were deserted and as they drove towards the farm Benton was excruciatingly aware of the sharp edge his headlights made against the falling snow, the humming of his tires on the snow-packed pavement.

"Has anything happened?"

"Nothing much," Benton said. For a moment, in a sudden burst of panic, Benton wondered if Thalia or Hartmann had written to Malcolm, begging him to rescue their friend from a fatal error.

"I met a lot of people," Totting said. "I think that's what made me better."

After a week, one afternoon when they were out walking through his farm, Benton told Totting about his affair with Robyn Marler.

"How did it end?" Totting asked.

"I just told her it was over," Benton said. Only that morning, he didn't bother to add, while he was at the university picking up a batch of essays. Robyn had come into his office, closed the door behind her, then stood nervously at his desk, gazing at the picture of Scott Fitzgerald. She looked unhappy. In fact, every day she was a little unhappier than the day before.

"I'm sorry," Benton found himself saying.

"It's not your fault."

"Let's give up now," Benton said, "while we can."

Robyn had turned away from him and walked out of the office. Remembering the sound of her leaving, Benton found that he had allowed his eyes to be filled by the sun. He blinked. In this bright light the white strands of Totting's hair lay like pale prisoners across his scalp. He looked like an old man; even his skin had started to separate into layers, like French pastry.

"Are you staying with Thalia?"

"I'm going to try."

"Love is the worst," Totting said.

Life on This Planet

When I first knew him, Brandt would come to visit me in the middle of the night. I was living the bachelor's life and would wake to the sound of his fist thudding insistently against the door of my house.

During the first winter, Brandt's visits always found me alone. Putting on my slippers and jeans I would open the door to discover Brandt in one of his states, invariably wearing the shapeless black overcoat he had adopted as his home, and often enough a fur hat crowned with a thick layer of snow. Beneath the coat and hat, Brandt was a shaggy mountain of flesh and thick black hair. His demonic emerald eyes were hooded by dense brows, his broad Slavic cheeks almost entirely covered by the dark Cossack beard that sprouted thickly from collarbone to cheekbone. Over his immense shoulders and matching gut Brandt wore a series of semi-identical cableknit sweaters. His trousers were thick and baggy corduroys churned out by some otherwise forgettable town in central Bulgaria.

I lived in a narrow one storey shack that filled the space between two more convincing houses. In fact my dwelling was, as Brandt often repeated, nothing more than an alleyway with a roof and two doors.

Sometimes, as Brandt shook himself doggily in the hall, clumps of snow from his coat would fall against my naked chest. Then Brandt would push me back with his mittened hand. "Who did you come to the door expecting, the craziest woman in the world?"

Meeting Brandt had coincided with the debacle of my latest attempt at civilized life with the opposite sex. My method of leaving the scene had been particularly dishonourable. In the midst of an argument the telephone had rung – a wrong number. After a suitable pause and double-take I had staggered towards the couch to announce that I had just learned my mother was fatally ill with cancer and that I must rush home to see her. Even while Brandt fed me scotch and cigarettes he had broken his "rule of privacy" and told me that I had better spend a year or two alone before inflicting myself once more on whatever poor innocent. "You see," Brandt said, "I don't need a magnifying glass to see that you hate women. I don't blame you, my friend, but even those you hate deserve politeness."

Brandt had a way with these terrible platitudes. He was so earnest and sincere that he even remembered his old ones and the circumstances under which he had trotted them out.

Brandt was a piano player.

Brandt's piano, a baby grand, took up most of his rented room and Brandt, seated on the bench during all visits, would interrupt his own sentences to dash off anything from a lightning classical cadenza to a spectacular series of jazz riffs.

Occasionally – though he could never be forced into it – Brandt would tell me to fill my glass and sit still. Then for an hour or more he would launch into musical free-association, bizarre medleys of every kind of tune and rhythm that sometimes broke into a recognizable piece of music, and other times stuttered with hysterical speed through the entire repertory of human noise.

His job was to provide supper music to a cheap *émigré* restaurant on Bloor Street. Every evening around ten the cult of his listeners would gather to hear Brandt's unpredictable musical monologue at the Neon Cellar Room. Brandt, wearing a tuxedo so shiny and moth-eaten that it seemed less formalwear than a costume with satiric intent, would bow to his listeners and commence with the Rachmaninoff-like series of chords that he had made his ironic signature.

Anyone else with Brandt's following would have known how to turn the admiration into money. Not Brandt. His small salary was almost entirely spent on the drinks he bought for himself and his female disciples. On this latter matter it must be said that Brandt proved himself a gentleman even by his own exacting standards.

Each of the assorted girls, young women, even damsels of a certain age, was accorded her fair share of drinks, cigarettes, and jokes; an increasing stream of small attentions which was almost universally crowned by a trip to the master's room – a trip which was never repeated.

What happened on these occasions I have no idea. After their evening with Brandt some never returned to hear him. Others, sentimentally drawn, came back night after night, patiently hoping that eventually their turn would come again.

"Men like you," Brandt said to me – meaning men who answered the door in jeans instead of brocaded pyjamas and housecoats; men who thought that where the flesh might wander, the heart must follow – "don't know anything about women. Women want to be cherished, not captured."

"You must have been reading Kahlil Gibran," I once accused him, after a particularly sincere discourse on the beauties of the pedestal.

"I never read books about love," Brandt said disdainfully. "Love must come *en direct*, from the heart."

It was Brandt's penchant for dropping French phrases that got him into trouble. The name of his nemesis was Claire

Boisvert or, as I came to call her, Claire Boisvert from Trois-Rivières. She was an actress, in fact, and she had achieved brief fame through a profile in the *Globe and Mail*. "Toronto's prettiest unemployed face," she was called, but so far as Brandt went she started the same as the others – sitting at a table with friends and listening to Brandt's fantasies. I myself, I must admit, bought her drinks on a couple of occasions, hoping something further might develop. I even walked her home once, but we stood so indecisively outside her door that eventually shaking hands seemed the only thing to do.

It was Brandt she wanted. One night, when he paused after a particularly startling series of melodic jumps, Claire called out "*Encore*." She had specialized in the Stanislavsky method. Brandt, never to be outdone, replied in French, sporting an accent that might have been stolen from a cavalry officer fresh from a starring role in *War and Peace*.

Soon after this exchange I left. At the time I was pretending to be a freelance journalist. After several semi-disastrous attempts at writing about the national economy, I had decided to convert myself into a travel writer by taking Spanish lessons. Unfortunately, I lacked the money to attend a language school. Instead, I spent an hour every night with a second-hand set of Berlitz records, reinforced by a once-weekly conversation with an old girlfriend who had once spent a month in Mexico.

I had already, the night Brandt and Claire began their fateful encounter, progressed to: "Excuse me, *señor*, I want to buy a red skirt."

It was, in fact, while listening to this sentence, drinking cheap Spanish wine and reading a travel folder about Yucatan that I fell into the deep sleep that Brandt interrupted. When I stumbled to my feet the record was clicking away in the final groove, and with my first step I kicked the wine glass across the room, leaving a pale pink highway across my fake oriental rug.

Brandt was in seventh heaven.

"I have to tell you," he said immediately. "Before I take off my coat I must announce that I, Brandt, have fallen in love."

"Take off your boots, too."

"Cynic," Brandt bellowed, "weak-blooded son of the bourgeoisie, love is what you have needed all along!"

Brandt strode into my living room and towered above my Spanish lessons like the entire Russian Army poised to invade a tiny principality.

"You know what I told her? 'Not like this,' I said, 'not like the others. Let me send you roses first.' " Brandt sighed. "And do you know what she said to me? *'C'est toi dont j'ai besoin.* I need you now.' "

"You have an international appeal," I said to Brandt. "What are you drinking tonight?"

"I have fallen in love with France," Brandt sighed. "Give me courvoisier, cognac, fabulous champagne."

"How about instant coffee?"

But Brandt could not be squelched. "I knew you would be unequal to true love. I have brought you something to help me celebrate." From the pocket of his coat he withdrew a silver flask. "*She* gave this to me," Brandt said. "It touched her lips, then mine. Please don't mind if I ask you to use a glass. In my old age I have discovered that I am jealous."

It was a week before I saw Brandt again. This time he wanted to invite me to dinner with Claire.

"You must arrive at six o'clock, so that you and Claire have a chance to know each other. And, if you don't mind my saying so, please dress for the occasion."

Suited up in the blazer and flannels I had used for interviewing captains of industry and commerce, and carrying a bottle of Hungarian red wine in memory of the Neon Cellar

Room, I showed up at Claire Boisvert's place as directed. Waiting for her to answer the doorbell I couldn't help remembering the crisp way she had shaken hands with me, as if one of us had just failed a crucial audition.

She answered the door wearing a gold brocade hostess gown and matching slippers. As I followed her up the stairs I wondered if she, like myself, had been instructed to appear in costume, or if this whole uncomfortable moment was her own theatrical inspiration. In the interview she had said that she had an inheritance from a maiden aunt in Paris. "*Tante* was an astrologer and a monarchist," Claire had declared, as if this would explain all.

Her living room was large and filled with the kind of furniture that is bought new, from furniture shoppes, with a colour scheme in mind. There was the sound of a piano playing – a wildly romantic rendition of Liszt – and as I sat down I saw that it was coming from a tape: Brandt immortalized.

"You were good for Brandt, I appreciate that."

Claire leaned forward to tell me this. Since starting up with Brandt she had become almost beautiful. Her black hair was cropped short, her complexion was all roses and cream, her mouth relaxed but sensuous. The large, doe-like eyes that had seemed overdone in the bar were, in her own home, soft and glowing.

"I mean," Claire said, "that men need to have friends when they're alone. Otherwise they grow bitter and twisted inside." She lit a cigarette with a gold lighter. I tried to imagine Brandt here, relaxing in the midst of what seemed to be a jewellery-store inspired decor, trading truths from the heart. This must be, I suddenly realized, the fulfilment of Brandt's wildest fantasy, the absolute opposite of his possession-less existence in the neo-Russian *émigré* boarding house, the apocalyptic moment of having conferred upon himself – in the glittering flesh of Claire Boisvert – his citizenship in the world of capitalism, show business, and democracy.

"You don't have to be afraid of me," Claire said. "I like you. You're shy, I can understand that. And you're afraid I'll take Brandt away from you." Out of a pocket in her gown she had produced a bottle opener. Now she popped the cork from the wine and filled the glasses she had set on the table between us.

"Men alone are like lovers with each other," Claire Boisvert said, "but they seldom have the courage to admit it. Of course you must be different. You're a writer, aren't you? Writers are always eager to confess."

"Not me," I said.

"You're different." Claire looked at me intently and I felt that somewhere, just offstage and out of my hearing, someone must be whispering her next line. "You try to make a joke out of everything but you're really a serious person. Brandt has told me all about you, but of course he only sees you from a man's point of view." She raised her glass. "To a long friendship," she proposed. We drank. "Listen," Claire said, "Brandt's kind of genius is easy to display. He simply sits down at the piano and everyone knows what he is. For a writer it's difficult, I know. You have no piano, only your own soul."

When Brandt arrived he was glowing with happiness. His cheeks were bright red with the cold – no doubt he had walked off miles of excitement – and when he kissed Claire he clasped his arms around her and squeezed her heartily.

"Now that you've gotten to know each other," Brandt said warmly, "we can have a wonderful evening." He sat down beside Claire and put his hand on her knee.

"You're one of a kind," Claire said.

About a month later Brandt announced that he and Claire were thinking of moving in together. His visits to me had slowed down, meanwhile, but not stopped entirely. In fact he came later and later – sometimes so wrought up after a meeting with Claire that he would spend the whole night pacing the snowy streets, arriving at my place in time to listen to the morning news and demand breakfast.

"We're going to look for a house," Brandt said, "big enough to hold my piano and Claire's books."

"Claire's books?"

"She is a very intelligent woman," said Brandt. "You don't see that about Claire right away, because she is so beautiful. But I would have no hesitation in saying that Claire is the most cultivated person I have ever met. There is no one whose opinion I respect more."

"And I thought you were only in love."

"You," Brandt said, "have never approved of this relationship. Claire tells me that you must be jealous. Is this true?"

I looked at Brandt across the loaf of Russian rye I kept especially for his visits. "I am jealous," I admitted. "I wish I were in love."

"You are in love too often," Brandt pronounced. "In any case, there is no point in your being jealous of that: when I am in love I am happy, but when you are in love you are miserable."

It was March. I wasn't in love but I was unhappy. Despite my Spanish lessons, I had not succeeded in persuading a magazine to send me south to research Spanish-speaking resort areas. But my nights with Berlitz had not been entirely in vain – I was working on an article about language schools. Every afternoon for a week, using different names, I went to various establishments of learning and had my linguistic abilities tested. Each reported to me that I was a genius, and that after a few months of daily private tuition I would be speaking like a native.

For these interviews, in order to appear plausible, I always dressed in my Captain of Commerce uniform. I would say that I was in the "import-export" business and needed to be able to talk to my contacts in their own language, so they would trust me.

The day following Brandt's announcement, the weather changed dramatically and it began to rain. The rain fell for six hours, long enough to triple the weight of the snow on my roof. Then the temperature plunged to record lows, converting the entire sodden mass to ice. When Brandt came to visit me the next night, water was dripping from my ceiling onto the manuscript of my educational experiences.

"You should move, too," Brandt said. "You and I and Claire could all live together."

"You said she doesn't like me."

"No," Brandt corrected me. "She said that you don't like her. She told me not to worry about it, that men always complain when their friends get married."

"Are you – "

Brandt beamed at me. "I have let the cat out of the bag. It was a secret. The ceremony was last week. But my landlady does not allow me to keep Claire overnight, and when I am in her apartment I grow lonely for my piano. So I still sleep at home. That is why we must find a place for both of us."

On the last day of March, the ceiling fell on my desk. Down with the plaster came chunks of rotted rafters, lumps of ice, a few shingles. I was woken up by the noise and rushed into my study to find the final re-type of my article on language schools buried under this undistinguished debris.

But before I could telephone my landlord, there was a hard banging at my front door. As I released the lock Brandt, wild-eyed and agitated, barged into the hall.

"What a terrible day," he groaned.

"Look," I said, pointing at my desk.

"You should get a cleaning lady," Brandt said. "You weren't meant to be a bachelor."

I followed him into the kitchen where he went straight for the brown closet where I kept my liquor.

"She left me." Brandt slumped down in the chair and his wide shoulders sagged. "She said that I was suffocating her. That I was like a huge cat torturing a tiny helpless mouse."

His eyes were bloodshot, and his voice cracked as he spoke. "When I tried to kiss her, she locked herself in the bathroom and called for the police." Brandt looked at me. "Can a man be put in jail for trying to kiss his own wife?" Before I could answer he brought his fist smashing down on the table. There was a loud crack as the oak board split, and at the sound I jumped, as if a rifle had been fired. Brandt was huge and powerful when he sat at the piano, but I had never thought of him as being physically violent. Now I wondered if, with Claire, he had indeed been threatening.

Brandt, too, leapt to his feet. He began pacing back and forth in the kitchen, his muscular hands wringing each other as if they wanted to tear the flesh right off the bones.

"What a bitch she is," Brandt said suddenly. "My life is ruined." He looked at me inquiringly, like a huge dog that has been caught in the flower bed and must now pay the catastrophic price. "I wish I could break her neck."

He had the bottle of scotch in his hands. To emphasize his point he wrenched off the cap and raised the bottle to his lips, taking an enormous gulp. Seconds later he was on his knees, gasping and choking.

"Brandt," I whispered, "Brandt, take it easy." I slapped him on the back as I repeated his name. By some miracle of physical dexterity he had retained his grasp on the bottle, which he raised to his mouth once more, this time with less disastrous effect. Then he rolled over on his back and lay on my kitchen floor, staring up at the ceiling like a gigantic beached whale.

"The first night," Brandt said, "when I brought her home, I treated her like the others. A woman wants to be cherished, not captured, who knows that better than I? I took her coat, turned the lights down, let her sit in the armchair while I played something on the piano. After a few minutes she stood up, put on her coat, and said: 'Heinrich, if I want to hear you play the piano I can listen to you at the Neon Cellar Room. Thank you for the concert, but my cat is waiting up for me. *Au revoir, mon cher*, in other words, goodbye.' Then she began to walk out the door. Why did I stop her? Because I was truly lonely that night, because I was sick of my landlady's cooking, because for months I had been thinking that my life must change or I would soon become an old man."

Brandt took a sip from the bottle but continued to speak directly to the lightbulb. "I stood up and apologized to her. I said that I had wanted to talk with her but I was shy in front of strangers. I offered her a drink. She reached into her coat pocket and out came a present in wrapping paper. With my name on it. 'I don't want to be like the others,' she said. 'Will you promise me that?' The gift was a bottle of brandy. We drank it together. I don't remember what we talked about – but then she turned out the light and said, 'Now, Brandt, I want to make love to you.' "

Brandt sat up on my kitchen floor and slid over so that his back was propped up by the refrigerator. Since the beginning of his affair with Claire he had been smoking French cigarettes. Now he pulled out a blue package of Gitanes: soon the room was clouded with dense smoke.

"I hate her," Brandt said. "Why did she have to pick me?"

It was early afternoon. I was still shovelling the ceiling into green garbage bags when the bell rang and the front door opened. I was expecting the landlord, so I didn't turn around until I heard Claire's voice.

Normally she wore makeup to emphasize her mouth and dark eyes – but today her eyelids and lips were swollen with crying, and she had brushed her hair straight back to expose a high, domed forehead. One of her hands was clutched round her purse, and in the other she held a white ox.

worried about Heinrich."

uld be, too, if I'd done to him what you have."

"And what have I done to him," Claire demanded angrily, "except to treat him as a human being."

At this point the landlord arrived. While he measured the ceiling and explained that many weeks would be required to make such an extensive repair, Claire sat in the kitchen. By the time the landlord had left and I had returned to her, she had made a pot of tea and set the table with cups and a pitcher of milk.

"I hope you don't mind."

"It was very nice of you," I said.

"I brought you a cake, too, from the bakery. I passed it on my way here." She took a plate from the counter – already the coffee cake was set out on it – and put it on the table between us. Before I could thank her she started to weep, silently, her eyes still open and looking into mine while tears trickled down her cheeks.

"I love him," Claire said. "From the very beginning I said to myself that I must remember there are special responsibilities when you get involved with a man of genius."

From the cupboard I took the bottle of scotch Brandt had been working on the night before. I poured Claire a drink, adding ice but no water: the same recipe she had requested the night I had approached her at the Neon Cellar Room.

"Thank you," Claire said. She tipped her glass back, emptied it in one swallow, then reached into her purse for cigarettes. "The worst thing for Heinrich is friends like you. Nothing personal. But if Heinrich does not grow up, then his musical genius will be wasted. Twenty years from now he will be a fat and pitiful drunk, stumbling over the keys. I don't want to save him, only to – " She paused.

"Rehabilitate him?"

This brought forth a new burst of tears. When she had

finished and dried her face, she lit another cigarette. "You're an ass," she said. "Yet you, and others like you, are what I have to contend with when I'm with Brandt. A few weeks ago I told him you should move in with us, when we get a house, so he would have you right there."

"Brandt told me you had gotten married."

Claire shook her head. "We exchanged rings, that's all. But I would have married him legally. We got a licence. Then Brandt confessed to me that he had been married before, when he lived in London. Of course I had expected something like that. Heinrich is the sort of person who scatters bits of himself, like discarded clothing, as he travels around. That is why I want to stay with Heinrich, because I know that after me he will never be able to fall in love again."

"And you?"

"You think I'm an idiot," Claire said. "But I am only honest. Heinrich Brandt is a genius. He is also a throwback. The Heinrich Brandt who takes care to appear so heroic in your eyes is not so used to the company of women."

"You're beginning to sound like a sex manual."

Claire blinked, tossed her head back as if she had been hit. "It's not that simple," she said. "Everything changes from one day to the next."

A few nights later Brandt came by. It was four in the morning, but his face was radiant. He and Claire had, he announced, decided to move in together. Into her apartment. His piano had already been transported and they had just signed a five year lease. The next night I was invited to dinner. Everything went smoothly and Claire made no reference to her visit to my house.

As I walked home it began to rain, a light spring drizzle. All the snow had melted, the smell of thawing earth was in the air. I found my steps beginning to accelerate, turn into a dance inspired by the sound of car tires whooshing along the wet asphalt. *Brandt and Claire*, the tires were singing, *Brandt and Claire from Trois-Rivières*. I stopped outside a store where I saw a display of copper pots for gourmet cooking. Recently my fortunes had been looking up, and the next morning, I vowed, I would buy these for Brandt and his newly resolved love, as a token of my belief in them, my sincere wishes for their lasting happiness.

I sent them the copper cookware and then it seemed that they dropped out of my life. At first I was busy and away a lot on assignment; then I realized it was several months since I'd dropped into the Neon Cellar Room to hear Brandt play.

One July night, after midnight, I went to see Brandt. He was behind the piano, dressed in his old black tuxedo jacket, now more moth-eaten than ever, his shirt open so that the hair from his massive chest sprang damply forth to meet his untrimmed beard.

Around the piano was Brandt's usual collection of admirers. His stubby fingers were tearing electrical jazz from the old upright. Feet were stamping, though it was a hot night, and in one crowded alleyway between the tables a couple was trying to dance.

After half an hour I got up to go. But Brandt saw me as I rose, and his glance caught mine, so I stayed until the end.

We walked away from the restaurant without speaking, my steps following Brandt's, always the leader. A blanket of cloud hung over the city, sealing in the summer warmth, and from the lake the smell of fish was slowly seeping northwards.

"She left me," Brandt said, as we turned into Claire's place. He opened the door and led me up the stairs. "She said she was going away for a couple of weeks to think things over, but then, after a month, she wrote me a letter explaining that she couldn't be my wife any longer, that she hadn't the courage to keep living with me. She told me that she would be away until the fall, when her rehearsals start for a new play. I haven't had the heart to move out yet."

Brandt slumped down into one of the chairs that had seemed so perfect during my first evening with Claire. The living room was a mass of dirty glasses, unwashed clothes; newspapers and magazines spread over furniture and carpets.

"This is the last I heard from her," Brandt said, handing me a postcard.

> Dear Heinrich,
> I am finding peace of mind at last. I think we are at some sort of crossroads but I wonder which is more important, our bodies or our minds. Anyway, I suppose both are contained by numerous other factors, including the energy of the universe. While in Yucatan I intend to spend time observing the stars and trying to reconcile myself to life on this planet.
>
> love,
> Claire Boisvert

"Look at the way she signs her name," Brandt said, as if she were in front of us signing it again and again. "Do you think she supposed I would forget it?"

He stood up, stretched, scooped his packet of Gitanes from the coffee table. "I told you she was brilliant," Brandt said. "Now I must find the courage that is in me, the strength to give her the freedom she needs. Wait and see. She will return my love and make me happy."

The Sins of Tomas Benares

A narrow, three storey house near College Street had been the home of the Benares family since they arrived in Toronto in 1936. Beside the front door, bolted to the brick, was a brass name-plate that was kept polished and bright: DR. TOMAS BENARES.

Benares had brought the name-plate – and little else – with him when he and his wife fled Spain just before the Civil War. For twenty years it had resided on the brick beside the doorway. And then, after various happinesses and tragedies – the tragedies being unfortunately more numerous – it had been replaced triumphantly by a new name-plate: DR. ABRAHAM BENARES. This son, Abraham, was the only child to have survived those twenty years.

Abraham had lost not only his siblings, but also his mother. The day his name-plate was proudly mounted Tomas could at last say to himself that perhaps his string of bad fortune had finally been cut, for despite everything he now had a son who was a doctor, like himself, and who was married with two children.

By 1960, the Benares household was wealthy in many ways. True, the family had not moved to the north of the city like many other immigrants who had made money, but during the era of the DR. ABRAHAM BENARES name-plate the adjoining house was purchased to give space for an expanded office and to provide an investment for Abraham Benares' swelling income as a famous internist. The back yards of both houses were combined into one elegant lawn that was tended twice a week by a professional gardener, an old Russian Jew who Tomas Benares had met first in his office, then at the synagogue. He spent most of his time drinking tea and muttering about the injustices that had been brought upon his people, while Tomas himself, by this time retired, toothless, and bent of back, crawled through the flower beds on his knees, wearing the discarded rubber dishwashing gloves of his son's extraordinarily beautiful wife.

Bella was her name. On anyone else, such a name would have been a joke; but Bella's full figure and dark, Mediterranean face glowed with such animal heat that from the first day he met her Tomas felt like an old man in her presence. Of this Bella seemed entirely unaware. After moving into the house she cooked for Tomas, pressed her scorching lips to his on family occasions, even hovered over him during meals, her fruity breath like a hot caress against his neck. After her children were born she began to refer to Tomas as grandfather, and sometimes while the infants played on the living room floor she would stand beside Tomas with the full weight of her fleshy hand sinking into his arm. "Look at us," she said to Tomas once, "three generations."

A few years after the birth of his daughter, Abraham Benares was walking with her down to College Street, as he did every Saturday, to buy a newspaper and a bag of apples, when a black Ford car left the street and continued its uncontrolled progress along the sidewalk where Abraham was walking. Instinctively, Abraham scooped Margaret into his arms, but the car was upon him before he could move. Abraham Benares, forty-one years old and the former holder of the city intercollegiate record for the one hundred yard dash, had time only to throw his daughter onto the adjacent lawn while the car mowed him down.

The next year, 1961, the name-plate on the door changed again: DR. TOMAS BENARES reappeared. There had been no insurance policy and the old man, now seventy-four years of age but still a licensed physician, recommenced the practice of medicine. He got the complaining gardener to redivide the yard with a new fence, sold the house next door to pay his son's debts, and took over the task of providing for his daughter-in-law and his two grandchildren.

Before reopening his practice, Tomas Benares got new false teeth and two new suits. He spent six months reading his old medical textbooks and walked several miles every morning to sweep the cobwebs out of his brain. He also, while walking, made it a point of honour never to look over his shoulder.

On the eve of his ninety-fourth birthday Tomas Benares was sixty-two inches tall and weighed one hundred and twelve pounds. These facts he noted carefully in a small diary. Each year, sitting in his third floor bedroom-study, Tomas Benares entered his height and weight into the pages of this diary. He also summarized any medical problems he had experienced during the year past, and made his prognosis for the year to come. There had once been an essay-like annual entry in which he confessed his outstanding sins and moral omissions from the previous year and outlined how he could correct or at least repent them in the year to follow. These essays had begun when Tomas was a medical student, and had continued well past the year in which his wife died. But when he had retired the first time from practising medicine and had the time to read over the fifty years of entries, he had noticed that his sins grew progressively more boring with age. And so, after that, he simply recorded the number of times he had enjoyed sexual intercourse that year.

Now, almost ninety-four, Tomas Benares couldn't help seeing that even this simple statistic had been absent for almost a decade. His diary was getting shorter while his life was getting longer. His last statistic had been when he was eighty-six – one time; the year before – none at all. But in his eighty-fourth year there had been a dozen transgressions. Transgressions! They should have been marked as victories. Tomas brushed back at the wisps of white hair that still adorned his skull. He couldn't remember feeling guilty or triumphant, couldn't remember any detail at all of the supposed events. Perhaps he had been lying. According to the entry, his height during that erotic year had been sixty-four inches, and his weight exactly twice that – one hundred and twenty-eight pounds. In 1956, when he had begun compiling the statistics, there had been only one admission of intercourse, but his height had been sixty-five inches and his weight one hundred and forty.

Suddenly, Tomas had a vision of himself as an old-fashioned movie. In each frame he was a different size, lived a different life. Only accelerating the reel could make the crowd into one person.

He was sitting in an old blue armchair that had been in the living room when Marguerita was still alive. There he used to read aloud in English to her, trying to get his accent right, while in the adjacent kitchen she washed up the dinner dishes and called out his mistakes. Now he imagined pulling himself out of the armchair, walking to the window to see if his grandson Joseph's car was parked on the street below. He hooked his fingers, permanently curved, into the arms of his chair. And then he pulled. But the chair was a vacuum sucking him down with the gravity of age. Beside him was a glass of raspberry wine. He brought it to his lips, wet the tip of his tongue. He was on that daily two-hour voyage between the departure of his day nurse and the arrival of Joseph. Eventually, perhaps soon, before his weight and height had entirely shrunk away and there were no statistics at all to enter into his diary, he would die. He wanted to die with the house empty. That was the last wish of Tomas Benares.

But even while his ninety-fourth birthday approached, Tomas Benares was not worrying about dying. To be sure he had become smaller with each year, and the prospect of worthwhile sin had almost disappeared; but despite the day nurse and the iron gravity of his chair, Tomas Benares was no invalid. Every morning this whole summer – save the week he had the flu – his nurse, whose name was Elizabeth Rankin, had helped him down the stairs and into the yard where, on his knees, he tended his gardens. While the front of the house had been let go by his careless grandson, Joseph, the back was preserved in the splendour it had known for almost fifty years. Bordering the carefully painted picket fence that surrounded the small yard were banks of flowers, the old strawberry patch, and in one corner a small stand of raspberry canes that were covered by netting to keep away the plague of thieving sparrows.

This morning, too, the morning of his birthday, Elizabeth Rankin helped him down the stairs. Elizabeth Rankin had strong arms, but although he could hardly walk down the three flights of stairs by himself – let alone climb back up – he could think of his own father, who had lived to be one hundred and twenty-three and of his grandfather Benares, who had lived to the same age. There was, in fact, no doubt that this enormous number was fate's stamp on the brow of the Benares men, though even fate could not *always* cope with automobiles.

But, as his own father had told Tomas, the Benares were to consider themselves blessed because fate seemed to pick them out more frequently than other people. For example, Tomas' father, who was born in 1820, had waited through two wives to have children, and when one was finally born, a boy, he had died of an unknown disease that winter brought to the Jewish quarter of Kiev. So frightened had he been by this show of God's spite that Tomas' father had sold the family lumbering business and rushed his wife back to Spain, the cradle of his ancestors, where she bore Tomas in 1884. Tomas' grandfather had, of course, been hale and hearty at the time: one hundred and four years old, he had lived on the top floor of the house just as Tomas now lived on the top floor of his own grandson's house.

That old man, Tomas' grandfather, had been a round, brown apple baked dry by the sun and surrounded by a creamy white fringe of beard. He had been born in 1780 and Tomas, bemoaning the emptiness of his diary on the occasion of his oncoming ninety-fourth, realized suddenly that he was holding two hundred years in his mind. His father had warned him: the Benares men were long-lived relics whose minds sent arrows back into the swamp of the past, so deep into the swamp that the lives they recalled were clamped together in a formless gasping mass, waiting to be shaped by those who remembered. The women were more peripheral: stately and beautiful they were easily extinguished; perhaps they were bored to death by the small, round-headed stubborn men who made up the Benares tribe.

"We were always Spaniards," the old man told Tomas, "stubborn as donkeys." *Stubborn as a donkey*, the child Tomas had whispered. Had his mother not already screamed this at him? And he imagined ancient Spain: a vast, sandy expanse where the Jews had been persecuted and in revenge had hidden their religion under prayer shawls and been stubborn as donkeys.

And they hadn't changed, Tomas thought gleefully, they hadn't changed at all; filled with sudden enthusiasm and the image of himself as a white-haired, virile donkey, he pulled himself easily out of his chair and crossed the room to the window where he looked down for Joseph's car. The room was huge: the whole third floor of the house save for an alcove walled off as a bathroom. Yet even in the afternoon the room was dark as a cave, shadowed by its clutter of objects that included everything from his marriage bed to the stand-up scale with the weights and sliding rule that he used to assess himself for his yearly entry.

From the window he saw that his grandson's car had yet to arrive. On the sidewalk instead were children travelling back and forth on tricycles, shouting to each other in a fractured mixture of Portugese and English. As always, when he saw children on the sidewalk, he had to resist opening the window and warning them to watch out for cars. It had been Margaret, only four years old, who had run back to the house to say that "Papa is sick," then had insisted on returning down the street with Tomas.

Two hundred years: would Margaret live long enough to sit frozen in a chair and feel her mind groping from one century to the next? Last year, on his birthday, she had given him the bottle of raspberry wine he was now drinking. "Every raspberry is a blessing," she had said. She had a flowery tongue, like her brother, and when she played music Tomas could sense her passion whirling like a dark ghost through the room. What would she remember? Her mother who had run away; her grandmother whom she had never known; her father, covered by a sheet by the time she and Tomas had arrived, blood from his crushed skull seeping into the white linen.

They had come a long way, the Benares: from the new Jerusalem in Toledo to two centuries in Kiev, only to be frightened back to Spain before fleeing again, this time to a prosperous city in the New World. But nothing had changed, Tomas thought, even the bitterness over his son's death still knifed through him exactly as it had when he saw

Margaret's eyes at the door, when Joseph, at the funeral, broke into a long, keening howl.

Stubborn as a donkey. Tomas straightened his back and walked easily from the window towards his chair. He would soon be ninety-four years old; and if fate was to be trusted, which it wasn't, there were to be thirty more years of anniversaries. During the next year, he thought, he had better put some effort into improving his statistics.

He picked up his diary again, flipped the pages backward, fell into a doze before he could start reading.

On his ninety-fourth birthday Tomas slept in. This meant not waking until after eight o'clock; and then lying in bed and thinking about his dreams. In the extra hours of sleep Tomas dreamed that he was a young man again, that he was married, living in Madrid, and that at noon the bright sun was warm as he walked the streets from his office to the *café* where he took lunch with his cronies. But in this dream he was not a doctor but a philosopher; for some strange reason it had been given to him to spend his entire life thinking about oak trees, and while strolling the broad, leafy streets it was precisely this subject that held his mind. He had also the duty, of course, of supervising various graduate students, all of whom were writing learned dissertations on the wonders of the oak; and it often, in this dream, pleased him to spend the afternoon with these bright and beautiful young people, drinking wine and saying what needed to be said.

In the bathroom, Tomas shaved himself with the electric razor that had been a gift from Joseph. Even on his own birthday he no longer trusted his hand with the straight razor that still hung, with its leather strop, from a nail in the wall. This, he suddenly thought, was the kind of detail that should also be noted in his annual diary – the texture of his shrinking world. Soon everything would be forbidden to him, and he would be left with only the space his own huddled skeleton could occupy. After shaving, Tomas washed his face, noting the exertion that was necessary just to open and close the cold water tap, and then he went back to the main room where he began slowly to dress.

It was true, he was willing to admit, that these days he often thought about his own death; but such thoughts did not disturb him. In fact, during those hours when he felt weak and sat in his chair breathing slowly, as if each weak breath might be his last, he often felt Death sitting with him. A quiet friend, Death; one who was frightening at first, but now was a familiar companion, an invisible brother waiting for him to come home.

But home, for Tomas Benares, was still the world of the living. When Elizabeth Rankin came to check on him, she found Tomas dressed and brushed. And a few minutes later he was sitting in his own garden, drinking espresso coffee and listening to the birds fuss in the flowering hedges that surrounded his patio. There Tomas, at peace, let the hot sun soak into his face. Death was with him in the garden, in the seductive buzz of insects, the comforting sound of water running in the nearby kitchen. The unaccustomed long sleep only gave Tomas the taste for more. He could feel himself drifting off, noted with interest that he had no desire to resist, felt Death pull his chair closer, his breath disguised as raspberries and mimosa.

At seventy-four years of age, also on his birthday, Tomas Benares had gone out to his front steps, unscrewed his son's name-plate and reaffixed his own. In the previous weeks he had restored the house to the arrangement it had known before his original retirement.

The front hall was the waiting room. On either side were long wooden benches, the varnished oak polished by a generation of patients. This front hall opened into a small parlour that looked onto the street. In that room was a desk, more chairs for waiting, and the doctor's files. At first his wife ran that parlour; after her death, Tomas had hired a nurse.

Behind the parlour was the smallest room of all. It had space for an examination table, a glass cabinet with a few books and several drawers of instruments, and a single uncomfortable chair. On the ceiling was a fluorescent light, and the window was protected by venetian blinds made of heavy plastic.

After Abraham's death his widow, Bella, and the children had stayed on in the Benares household, and so on the morning of the reopening Tomas had gone into the kitchen to find Bella making coffee and feeding breakfast to Joseph and Margaret. He sat down wordlessly at the kitchen table while Bella brought him coffee and toast, and he was still reading the front section of the morning paper when the doorbell rang. Joseph leapt from the table and ran down the hall. Tomas was examining the advertisement he had placed to announce the recommencement of his practice.

"Finish your coffee," said Bella. "Let her wait. She's the one who needs the job."

But Tomas was already on his feet. Slowly he walked down the hall to the front parlour. He could hear Joseph chatting with the woman, and was conscious of trying to keep his back straight. He was wearing, for his new practice, a suit newly tailored. His old tailor had died, but his son had measured Tomas with the cloth tape, letting his glasses slide down to rest on the tip of his nose exactly like his father had. Now in his new blue suit, a matching tie, and one of the white linen shirts that Marguerita had made for him, Tomas stood in his front parlour.

"Doctor Benares, I am Elizabeth Rankin; I answered your advertisement for a nurse."

"I am pleased to meet you, Mrs. Rankin."

"Miss Rankin." Elizabeth Rankin was then a young woman entering middle age. She had brown hair parted in the middle and then pulled back in a bun behind her neck, eyes of a darker brown in which Tomas saw a mixture of fear and sympathy. She was wearing a skirt and a jacket, but had with her a small suitcase in case it was necessary for her to start work right away.

"Would you like to see my papers, Doctor Benares?"
"Yes, if you like. Please sit down."

Joseph was still in the room and Tomas let him watch as Elizabeth Rankin pulled out a diploma stating that she had graduated from McGill University in the biological sciences, and another diploma showing that she had received her RN from the same university.

"I have letters of reference, Doctor Benares."
"Joseph, please get a cup of coffee for Miss Rankin. Do you – "
"Just black, Joseph."

They sat in silence until Joseph arrived with the coffee, and then Tomas asked him to leave and closed the door behind him.

"I'm sorry," Elizabeth Rankin said. "I saw the advertisement and . . ."

She trailed off. It was six months since Tomas had seen her, but he recognized her right away; she was the woman who had been driving the car that had killed his son. At the scene of the accident she had shivered in shock until the ambulance arrived. Tomas had even offered her some sleeping pills. Then she had reappeared to hover on the edge of the mourners at Abraham's funeral.

"You're a very brave woman, Miss Rankin."
"No, I . . ." Her eyes clouded over. Tomas, behind the desk, watched her struggle. When he had seen her in the hall, his first reaction had been anger.

"I thought I should do something," she said. "I don't need a salary, of course, and I *am* a qualified nurse."

"I see that," Tomas said dryly.

"You must hate me," Elizabeth Rankin said.

Tomas shrugged. Joseph came back into the room and stood beside Elizabeth Rankin. She put her hand on his shoulder and the boy leaned against her.

"You mustn't bother Miss Rankin," Tomas said, but even as he spoke he could see Elizabeth's hand tightening on the boy's shoulder.

"Call Margaret," Tomas said to Joseph, and then asked himself why, indeed, he should forgive this woman. No reason came to mind, and while Joseph ran through the house, searching for his sister, Tomas sat in his reception room and looked carefully at the face of Elizabeth Rankin. The skin below her eyes was dark, perhaps she had trouble sleeping; and though her expression was maternal she had a tightly drawn quality that was just below the surface, as though the softness were a costume.

He remembered a friend, who had been beaten by a gang of Franco's men, saying he felt sorry for them. When Tomas' turn came, he had felt no pity for his assailants. And although what Elizabeth Rankin had done was an accident, not a malicious act, she was still the guilty party. Tomas wondered if she knew what he was thinking, wondered how she could not. She was sitting with one leg crossed over the other, her eyes on the door through which the sounds of the children's feet now came. And when Margaret, shy, sidled into the room, Tomas made a formal introduction. He was thinking, as he watched Margaret's face, how strange it was that the victims must always console their oppressors.

Margaret, four years old, curtsied and then held out her hand. There was no horrified scream, no flicker of recognition.

"Miss Rankin will be coming every morning," Tomas announced. "She will help me in my office."

"You are very kind, Doctor Benares."

"We will see," Tomas said. It was then that he had an

extraordinary thought, or at least a thought that was extraordinary for him. It occurred to him that Elizabeth Rankin didn't simply want to atone, or to be consoled. She wanted to be taken advantage of.

Tomas waited until the children had left the room, then closed the door. He stood in front of Elizabeth Rankin until she, too, got to her feet.

"Pig," Tomas Benares hissed; and he spat at her face. The saliva missed its target and landed, instead, on the skin covering her right collarbone. There it glistened, surrounded by tiny beads, before gliding down the open V of her blouse.

The eyes of Elizabeth Rankin contracted briefly. Then their expression returned to a flat calm. Tomas, enraged, turned on his heel and walked quickly out of the room. When he came back fifteen minutes later, Elizabeth Rankin had changed into her white uniform and was sorting through the files of his son.

Bella said it wasn't right.

"That you should have *her* in the house," she said. "It's disgusting."

"She has a diploma," Tomas said.

"And how are you going to pay her? You don't have any patients."

This discussion took place in the second floor sitting room after the children were asleep. It was the room where Bella and Abraham used to go to have their privacy.

"At first I thought maybe you didn't recognize her," Bella started again, "and so I said to myself, what sort of a joke is this? Maybe she didn't get enough the first time, maybe she has to come back for more."

"It was an accident," Tomas said.

"So you forgive her?" Bella challenged. She had a strong, bell-like voice which, when she and Abraham were first married, had been a family joke, one even she would laugh at; but since his death the tone had grown rusty and sepulchral.

Tomas shrugged.

"I don't forgive her," Bella said.

"It was an accident," Tomas said. "She has to work it out of her system."

"What about me? How am I going to work it out of my system?"

At thirty, Bella was even more beautiful than when she had been married. The children had made her heavy, but grief had carved away the excess flesh. She had jet-black hair and olive skin that her children had both inherited. Now she began to cry and Tomas, as always during these nightly outbursts of tears, went to stand by the window.

"Well?" Bella insisted. "What do you expect me to do?"

When she had asked this question before, Tomas advised her to go to sleep with the aid of a pill. But now he hesitated. For how many months, for how many years could he tell her to obliterate her evenings in sleeping pills.

"You're the saint," Bella said. "You never wanted anyone after Marguerita."

"I was lucky," Tomas said. "I had a family."

"I have a family."

"I was older," Tomas said.

"So," Bella repeated dully, "you never did want anyone else."

Tomas was silent. When Abraham brought her home he had asked Tomas what he thought of her. "She's very beautiful," Tomas had said. Abraham had happily agreed. Now she was more beautiful but, Tomas thought, also more stupid.

"It is very hard," Tomas said, "for a man my age to fall in love."

"Your wife died many years ago . . ."

Tomas shrugged. "I always felt old," he said, "ever since

we came to Canada." All this time he had been standing at the window, and now he made sure his back was turned so that she wouldn't see his tears. The day Abraham had been killed he had cried with her. Since then, even at the funeral, he had refused to let her see his tears. Why? He didn't know. The sight of her, even the smell of her walking into a room, seemed to freeze his heart.

"If there was – " Bella started. She stopped. Tomas knew that he should help her, that she shouldn't have to fight Abraham's ghost *and* his father, but he couldn't bring himself to reach out. It was like watching an ant trying to struggle its way out of a pot of honey.

"If there was someone else," Bella said. "Even a job."

"What can you do?" Tomas asked, but the question was rhetorical; Bella had married Abraham the year after she had finished high school. She couldn't even type.

"*I* could be your receptionist, instead of that – "

"Nurse," Tomas interrupted. "I need a nurse, Bella."

"I can put a thermometer in someone's mouth," Bella said. "Are people going to die while you're next door in the office?"

"A doctor needs a nurse," Tomas said. "I didn't invent the rules."

"There's a rule?"

"It's a custom, Bella."

He turned from the window.

"And anyway," Bella said, "who's going to take care of the children?"

"That's right, the children need a mother."

"We need Bella in the kitchen making three meals a day so at night she can cry herself to sleep – while the murderer is working off her guilt so at night she can go out and play with the boys, her conscience clean."

"You don't know what she does at night – "

"You're such a saint," Bella said suddenly. "You are such a saint the whole world admires you, do you know that?"

"Bella – "

"The holy Doctor Benares. At seventy-four years of age he ends his retirement and begins work again to provide for his widowed daughter and his two orphaned grandchildren. Has the world ever seen such a man? At the *shul* they're talking about adding a sixth book to the Torah." She looked at Tomas, and Tomas, seeing her go out of control, could only stand and watch. She was like an ant, he was thinking. Now the ant was at the lip of the pot. It might fall back into the honey, in which case it would drown; or it might escape after all.

"You're such a saint," Bella said in her knife-edge voice, "you're such a saint that you think poor Bella just wants to go out and get laid."

She was teetering on the edge now, Tomas thought.

"You should see your face now," Bella said. "*Adultery*, you're thinking. *Whore.*"

"It's perfectly normal for a healthy—"

"Oh, healthy *shit!*" Bella screamed. "I just want to go out. Out, out, *out!*"

She was standing in the doorway, her face beet-red, panting with her fury. Tomas, staying perfectly still, could feel his own answering blush searing the backs of his ears, surrounding his neck like a hot rope.

"Even the saint goes for a walk," Bella's voice had dropped again. "Even the saint can spend the afternoon over at Herman Levine's apartment, playing cards and drinking beer."

Tomas could feel his whole body burning and chafing inside his suit. *The saint*, she was calling him. And what had he done to her? Offered her and her family a home when they needed it. "Did I make Abraham stay here?" Tomas asked. And then realized, to his shame, that he had said the words aloud.

He saw Bella in the doorway open her mouth until it looked like the muzzle of a cannon. Her lips struggled and convulsed. The room filled with unspoken obscenities.

Tomas reached a hand to touch the veins in his neck.

They were so engorged with blood he was choking. He tore at his tie, forced his collar open.

"Oh, God," Bella moaned.

Tomas was coughing, trying to free his throat and chest. Bella was in the corner of his hazed vision, staring at him in the same detached way he had watched her only a few moments before.

The saint, Tomas was thinking, *she calls me the saint*. An old compartment of his mind suddenly opened, and he began to curse at her in Spanish. Then he turned his back and walked upstairs to his third floor bedroom.

In the small hours of the morning, Tomas Benares was lying in the centre of his marriage bed, looking up at the ceiling of the bedroom and tracing the shadows with his tired eyes. These shadows: cast by the streetlights they were as much a part of his furniture as was the big oak bed, or the matching dressers that presided on either side – still waiting, it seemed, for the miraculous return of Marguerita.

As always he was wearing pyjamas – sewing had been another of Marguerita's talents – and like the rest of his clothes they had been cleaned and ironed by the same Bella who had stood in the doorway of the second floor living room and bellowed and panted at him like an animal gone mad. The windows were open and while he argued with himself Tomas could feel the July night trying to cool his skin, soothe him. But he didn't want to be soothed, and every half hour or so he raised himself on one elbow and reached for a cigarette, flaring the light in the darkness and feeling for a second the distant twin of the young man who had lived in Madrid forty years ago, the young man who had taken lovers (all of them beautiful in retrospect), whispered romantic promises (all of them ridiculous), and then had the good fortune to fall in love and marry a woman so beautiful and devoted that even his dreams could never have imagined her. And yet it was true, as he had told Bella, that when he came to Canada his life had ended. Even lying with Marguerita in this bed he had often been unable to sleep, had often, with this very gesture, lit up a small space in the night in order to feel close to the young man who had been deserted in Spain.

Return? Yes, it had occurred to him after the war was finished. Of course, Franco was still in power then, but it was his country and there were others who had returned. And yet, what would have been the life of an exile returned? The life of a man keeping his lips perpetually sealed, his thoughts to himself; the life of a man who had sold his heart in order to have the sights and smells that were familiar.

Now, Tomas told himself wryly, he was an old man who had lost his heart for nothing at all. Somehow, over the years, it had simply disappeared; like a beam of wood being eaten from the inside, it had dropped away without him knowing it.

Tomas Benares, on his seventy-fourth birthday, had just put out a cigarette and lain back with his head on the white linen pillow to resume his study of the shadows, when he heard the footsteps on the stairs up to his attic. Then there was the creak of the door opening and Bella, in her nightgown and carrying a candle, tiptoed into the room.

Tomas closed his eyes.

The footsteps came closer, he felt the bed sag with her weight. He could hear her breathing in the night, it was soft and slow; and then, as he realized he was holding his own breath, he felt Bella's hand come to rest on his forehead.

He opened his eyes. In the light of the candle her face was like stone, etched and lined with grief.

"I'm sorry," Tomas said.

"I'm the sorry one. And imagine, on your birthday."

"That's all right. We've been too closed-in here, since –"

Here he hesitated, because for some reason the actual event was never spoken. "Since Abraham died."

Bella now took her hand away, and Tomas was aware of how cool and soft it had been. Sometimes, decades ago, Marguerita had comforted him in this same way when he couldn't sleep. Her hand on his forehead, fingers stroking his cheeks, his eyes, soothing murmurs until finally he drifted away, a log face-down in the cool water.

"There are still lives to be lived," Bella was saying. "The children."

"The children," Tomas repeated. Not since Marguerita had there been a woman in this room at night. For many years he used to lock the door when he went to bed, and even now he would still lock it on the rare times he was sick in case someone – who? – should dare to come on a mission of mercy.

"I get tired," Bella said. Her head drooped and Tomas could see, beyond the outline of her nightdress, the curve of her breasts, the fissure between. A beautiful woman, he had thought before . . . . He was not as saintly as Bella imagined. On certain of the afternoons Bella thought he was at Herman Levine's, Tomas had been visiting a different apartment, that of a widow who was once his patient. She, too, knew what it was like to look at the shadows on the ceiling for one year after another, for one decade after another.

Now Tomas reached out for Bella's hand. Her skin was young and supple, not like the skin of the widow, or his own. There came a time in every person's life, Tomas thought, when the inner soul took a look at the body and said: Enough, you've lost what little beauty you had and now you're just an embarrassment – I'll keep carrying you around, but I refuse to take you seriously. Tomas, aside from some stray moments of vanity, had reached that point long ago; but Bella, he knew, was still in love with her body, still wore her own bones and skin and flesh as a proud inheritance and not an aging inconvenience.

"Happy birthday," Bella said. She lifted Tomas' hand and pressed it to her mouth. At first, what he felt was the wetness of her mouth. And then it was her tears that flowed in tiny, warm streams around his fingers.

She blew out the candle at the same time that Tomas reached for her shoulder; and then he drew her down so she was lying beside him – her on top of the covers and him beneath, her thick, jet hair folded into his neck and face, her perfume and the scent of her mourning skin wrapped around him like a garden. Chastely he cuddled her to him, her warm breath as soothing as Marguerita's had once been. He felt himself drifting into sleep, and he turned towards the perfume, the garden, turned towards Bella to hold her in his arms the way he used to hold Marguerita in that last exhausted moment of waking.

Bella shifted closer, herself breathing so slowly that Tomas thought she must be already asleep. He remembered, with relief, that his alarm was set for six o'clock; at least they would wake before the children. Then he felt his own hand, as if it had a life of its own, slide in a slow caress from Bella's shoulder to her elbow, touching, in an accidental way, her sleeping breast.

Sleep fled at once, and Tomas felt the sweat spring to his skin. Yet Bella only snuggled closer, breasts and hips flooding through the blanket like warm oceans. Tomas imagined reaching for and lighting a cigarette, the darkness parting once more. A short while ago he had been mourning his youth and now, he reflected, he was feeling as stupid as he ever had. Even with the widow there had been no hesitation. Mostly on his visits they sat in her living room and drank tea; sometimes, by a mutual consent that was arrived at without discussion, they went to her bedroom and performed sex like a warm and comfortable bath. A bath, he thought to himself, that was how he and Bella should become; chaste, warm, comforts to each other in the absence of Abraham. It wasn't right, he now decided, to have frozen his heart to this woman – his daughter-in-law, after all;

surely she had a right to love, to the warmth and affection due to a member of the family. *Bella,* he was ready to proclaim, *you are the mother of my grandchildren, the chosen wife of my son. And if you couldn't help shouting, at least you were willing to comfort me.*

Tomas held Bella closer. Her lips, he became aware, were pressed against the hollow of his throat, moving slowly, kissing the skin and now sucking gently at the hairs that curled up from his chest. Tomas let his hand find the back of her neck. There was a delicate valley that led down from her skull past the thick, black hair. He would never have guessed she was built so finely.

Now Bella's weight lifted away for a moment, though her lips stayed glued to his throat, and then suddenly she was underneath the covers, her leg across his groin, her hand sliding up his chest.

Tomas felt something inside of him break. And then, as he raised himself on top of Bella the night, too, broke open; a gigantic black and dreamless mouth, it swallowed them both. He kissed her, tore at her nightgown to suck at her breast, penetrated her so deeply that she gagged; yet though he touched and kissed her every private place; though they writhed on the bed and he felt the cool sweep of her lips as they searched out his every nerve; though he even opened his eyes to see the pleasure on her face, her black hair spread like dead butterflies over Marguerita's linen pillows, her mouth open with repeated climax, the night still swallowed them, obliterated everything as it happened, took them rushing down its hot and endless gorge until Tomas felt like Jonah in the belly of the whale; felt like Jonah trapped in endless flesh and juice. And all he had to escape with was his own sex: like an old sword he brandished it in the blackness, pierced open tunnels, flailed it against the wet walls of his prison.

"Bella, Bella, Bella." He whispered her name silently. Every time he shaped his lips around her name, he was afraid the darkness of his inner eye would part, and Abraham's face would appear before him. But it didn't happen. Even as he scratched Bella's back, bit her neck, penetrated her from behind, he taunted himself with the idea that somewhere in this giant night Abraham must be waiting. His name was on Tomas' lips: Abraham his son. How many commandments was he breaking? Tomas wondered, pressing Bella's breasts to his parched cheeks.

Tomas felt his body, like a starved man at a banquet, go out of control. Kissing, screwing, holding, stroking: everything he did Bella wanted, did back, invented variations upon. For one brief second he thought that Marguerita had never been like this, then his mind turned on itself and he was convinced that this *was* Marguerita, back from the dead with God's blessing to make up, in a few hours, a quarter century of lost time.

But as he kissed and cried over his lost Marguerita, the night began to lift and the first light drew a grey mask on the window.

By this time he and Bella were lying on their stomachs, side by side, too exhausted to move.

The grey mask began to glow, and as it did Tomas felt the dread rising in him. Surely God Himself would appear to take His revenge, and with that thought Tomas realized he had forgotten his own name. He felt his tongue searching, fluttering between his teeth, tasting again his own sweat and Bella's fragrant juices. He must be, he thought, in Hell. He had died and God, to drive his wicked soul crazy, had given him this dream of his own daughter-in-law, his dead son's wife.

"Thank you, Tomas."

No parting kiss, just soft steps across the carpet and then one creak as she descended the stairs. Finally, the face of his son appeared. It was an infant's face, staring uncomprehendingly at its father.

Tomas sat up. His back was sore, his kidneys felt trampled, one arm ached, his genitals burned. He stood up to go to the bathroom and was so dizzy that for a few moments he had to cling to the bedpost with his eyes closed. Then, limping and groaning, he crossed the room. When he got back to the bed there was no sign that Bella had been there – but the sheets were soaked as they sometimes were after a restless night.

He collapsed on the covers and slept dreamlessly until the alarm went off. When he opened his eyes his first thought was of Bella, and when he swung out of bed there was a sharp sting in his groin. But as he dressed he was beginning to speculate, even to hope, that the whole episode had been a dream.

A few minutes later, downstairs at breakfast, Tomas found the children sitting alone at the table. Between them was a sealed envelope addressed to "Dr. Tomas Benares, M.D."

"Dear Tomas," the letter read, "I have decided that it is time for me to seek my own life in another city. Miss Rankin has already agreed to take care of the children for as long as necessary. I hope you will all understand me and remember that I love you. As always, Bella Benares."

On his birthday, his garden always seemed to reach that explosive point that marked the height of summer. No matter what the weather, it was this garden that made up for all other deprivations, and the fact that his ninety-fourth birthday was gloriously warm and sunny made it doubly perfect for Tomas to spend the day outside.

Despite the perfect blessing of the sky, as Tomas opened his eyes from that long doze that had carried the sun straight into the afternoon, he felt a chill in his blood, the knowledge that Death, that companion he'd grown used to, almost fond of, was starting to play his tricks. Because sitting in front of him, leaning towards him as if the worlds of waking and sleeping had been forced together, was Bella herself.

"Tomas, Tomas, it's good to see you. It's Bella."

"I know," Tomas said. His voice sounded weak and grumpy; he coughed to clear his throat.

"Happy birthday, Tomas."

He pushed his hand across his eyes to rid himself of this illusion.

"Tomas, you're looking so good."

Bella: her face was fuller now, but the lines were carved deeper, bracketing her full lips and corrugating her forehead. And yet she was still young, amazing: her movements were lithe and supple; her jet-black hair was streaked, but still fell thick and wavy to her shoulders; her eyes still burned, and when she leaned forward to take his hand between her own the smell of her, dreams and remembrances, came flooding back.

"Tomas, are you glad to see me?"

"You look so young, Bella." This in a weak voice, but Tomas' throat-clearing cough was lost in the rich burst of Bella's laughter. Tomas, seeing her head thrown back and the flash of her strong teeth, could hardly believe that he, a doddering old man, whose knees were covered by a blanket in the middle of summer, had only a few years ago actually made love to this vibrant woman. Now she was like a racehorse in voracious maturity.

"Bella, the children."

"I know, Tomas. I telephoned Margaret; she's here. And I telephoned Joseph, too. His secretary said he was at a meeting all afternoon, but that he was coming here for dinner."

"Bella, you're looking wonderful, truly wonderful." Tomas had his hand hooked into hers and, suddenly aware that he was half-lying in his chair, was using her weight to try to lever himself up.

Instantly Bella was on her feet, her arm solicitously around his back, pulling him into position. She handled his weight, Tomas thought, like the weight of a baby. He felt surrounded by her, overpowered by her smell, her vitality, her cheery goodwill. *Putan*, Tomas whispered to himself. What a revenge. Twenty years ago he had been her equal; and now, suddenly – what had happened? Death was in the garden; Tomas could feel his presence, the familiar visitor turned trickster. And then Tomas felt some of his strength returning, strength in the form of contempt for Bella, who had waited twenty years to come back to this house; contempt for Death, who waited until a man was an ancient, drooling husk to test his will.

"You're the marvel, Tomas. Elizabeth says you work every day in the garden. How do you do it?"

"I spit in Death's face," Tomas rasped. Now he was beginning to feel more himself again, and he saw that Bella was offering him a cup of coffee. All night he had slept, and then again in the daytime. What a way to spend a birthday! But coffee would heat the blood, make it run faster. He realized that he was famished.

Bella had taken out a package of cigarettes now, and offered one to Tomas. He shook his head, thinking again how he had declined in these last years. Now Joseph wouldn't let him smoke in bed, even when he couldn't sleep. He was only allowed to smoke when there was someone else in the room, or when he was outside in the garden.

"Tomas. I hope you don't mind I came back. I wanted to see you again while – while we could still talk."

Tomas nodded. So the ant had escaped the honey pot after all, and ventured into the wide world. Now it was back, wanting to tell its adventures to the ant who had stayed home. Perhaps they hadn't spent that strange night making love after all; perhaps in his bed they had been struggling on the edge of the pot, fighting to see who would fall back and who would be set free.

"So," Bella said. "It's been so long."

Tomas, watching her, refusing to speak, felt control slowly moving towards him again. He sat up straighter, brushed the blanket off his legs.

"Or maybe we should talk tomorrow," Bella said, "when you're feeling stronger."

"I feel strong." His voice surprised even himself – not the weak squawk it sometimes was now, a chicken's squeak hardly audible over the telephone, but firm and definite, booming out of his chest the way it used to. Bella: she had woken him up once, perhaps she would once more.

He could see her moving back, hurt; but then she laughed again, her rich throaty laugh that Tomas used to hear echoing through the house when his son was still alive. He looked at her left hand; Abraham's modest engagement ring was still in place, but beside it was a larger ring, a glowing bloodstone set in a fat gold band. "Tomas," Bella was saying, "you really are a marvel, I swear you're going to live to see a hundred."

"One hundred and twenty-three," Tomas said. "Almost all of the Benares men live to be one hundred and twenty-three."

For a moment, the lines deepened again in Bella's face, and Tomas wished he could someday learn to hold his tongue. A bad habit that should have long ago been entered in his diary.

"You will," Bella finally said. Her voice had the old edge. "*Two* hundred and twenty-three, you'll dance on all our graves."

"Bella."

"I shouldn't have come."

"The children – "

"They'll be glad to see me, Tomas, they always are."

"Always?"

"Of course. Did you think I'd desert my own children?" Tomas shook his head.

"Oh, I left, Tomas, I left. But I kept in touch. I sent them letters and they wrote me back. That woman helped me."

"Elizabeth?"

"I should never have called her a murderer, Tomas. It was an accident."

"They wrote you letters without telling me?"

Bella stood up. She was a powerful woman now, full-fleshed and in her prime; even Death had slunk away in the force of her presence. "I married again, Tomas. My husband and I lived in Seattle. When Joseph went to university there, he lived in my home."

"Joseph lived with you?"

"My husband's dead now, Tomas, but I didn't come for your pity. Or your money. I just wanted you to know that I would be in Toronto again, seeing my own children, having a regular life."

"A regular life," Tomas repeated. He felt dazed, dangerously weakened. Death was in the garden again, he was standing behind Bella, peeking out from behind her shoulders and making faces. He struggled to his feet. Only Bella could save him now, and yet he could see the fear on her face as he reached for her.

"Tomas, I–"

"You couldn't kill me!" Tomas roared. His lungs filled his chest like an eagle in flight. His flowering hedges, his roses, his carefully groomed patio snapped into focus. He stepped towards Bella, his balance perfect, his arm rising. He saw her mouth open, her lips begin to flutter. Beautiful but stupid, Tomas thought; some things never change. At his full height he was still tall enough to put his arm around her and lead her to the house.

"It's my birthday." His voice boomed with the joke. "Let me offer you a drink to celebrate your happy return."

His hand slid from her shoulder to her arm; the skin was smooth as warm silk. Her face turned towards his: puzzled, almost happy, and he could feel the heat of her breath as she prepared to speak.

"Of course I forgive you," Tomas said.

Death of a Guppy

My mother had a job supervising the care of underprivileged children, so to ease the burden of housework she hired a cleaning lady to come once a week. Her name was Mrs. Lusk, though that was not what we called her.

This was during the era of my family's relative prosperity, when we had moved to a four bedroom house in Ottawa West. I was attending high school then, one which placed a strong emphasis on mental health. In grade ten, for example, we were required to write an essay on the hazards of marijuana. At the time I was thirteen years old and had never even tasted coffee; nonetheless my essay received an A minus. According to the Health instructor, who was actually the basketball coach, marijuana cigarettes – reefers – were sold in a place called Seed's Billiard Hall. I had often passed this terrifying place, known to be the haunt of certain senior students. By the door were often clustered a few men, out-of-work, wearing baggy flannel pants and beige wind-breakers. They showed none of the symptoms of Reefer Madness, as our Health teacher called it, nor even of those horrible cancers I had described with such telling effect in my essay.

Among the cleaning lady's tasks were doing the washing and the ironing. One afternoon she suggested that my brother and I take our trousers off so she could press them, too. After that we called her Mrs. Lust.

Mrs. Lust had a boyfriend who ate lunch at Seed's. In the afternoons – after school but before my mother came home from her missions of mercy – he would park his maroon-finned Chevrolet in front of our house and visit Mrs. Lust, whose husband never appeared but sometimes telephoned in a thick, beery voice. The boyfriend was tall and slack-bellied. He wore a Canadian Tire Hockey Team wind-breaker, and his straight black hair was slicked back into a ducktail. We liked him. However, he never offered us a cigarette, filled with marijuana or otherwise, so at this time in our lives we were entirely free from the perils of drug addiction. In fact, the boyfriend – whose name was never spoken, possibly for reasons of discretion – had only one mania: this was for hot dogs well-slathered in mustard. He would often buy them by the dozen to take out – ready-cooked and in soft, white buns – and bring them to the house. They would be shared out among himself, my brother and myself, Mrs. Lust, and our budgie, whose name was Benny.

Benny was not the only budgie in the neighbourhood. The girl next door had one. Her mother was a widow and her budgie could say "Bye-bye" if it was fed potato chips. Our budgie couldn't say anything, and that is why we started to give it bits of hot dog. These caused the budgie's feathers to fall out; and in addition – possibly it will one day be discovered that as far as budgies go, mustard is a powerful drug – Benny became very neurotic. So pronounced grew Benny's depressions that my father noticed them. Every evening when he came home he would let Benny out, and Benny would fly to the drapes where he would perch briefly, flutter his featherless wings, and go to the bathroom.

To keep up the family morale we decided to get a guppy. We had already tried a dog, in a previous house and era, but the dog – a boxer – so frightened my mother with the insistent sounds it made from its de-barked larynx that it was returned to the veterinarian. This veterinarian's son was famous for doing backflips, and later became very successful.

We bought the guppy one Saturday afternoon at a downtown pet shop. There was a whole outfit involved: an aquarium with metal reinforced corners, genuine white sand, plants imported from the Caribbean, an automatic filter that bubbled oxygen through the de-chlorinated water. After the problems with Benny, a happy childhood had been planned for Gilbert the guppy. There were even other fish to be his playmates, but Gilbert was the only guppy, and the only fish with a name. Translucent but not see-through, distinguished by two perfectly round blue dots on his tail and by his intelligent brown eyes, Gilbert won our hearts from the beginning.

"It's a terrible shame about your bird," Mrs. Lust would always say. "Birds should never be in cages." But about the fish she had no such moral hesitation. No one knew the natural habitat of guppies, and I was in no hurry to search it out in the encyclopaedia.

After we had had Gilbert for about a month, Mrs. Lust changed boyfriends. The ironing incident had made anything possible, so I asked her what had happened. Mrs. Lust burst into tears and said that men were all of a type, and that she hoped I would be different but I wouldn't. Seeing her face all red and streaked with emotion I felt like crying myself. Before Mrs. Lust there had been another babysitter: a seventy-five-year-old woman called – by herself, even – Mrs. Moulds. When we were promoted to Mrs. Lust we had accepted the change with difficulty, but now, faced with actual tears, I had the sudden unwanted insight that Mrs. Lust was the adult version of the children to whom my mother had devoted her career.

By now, in Health class, we had written essays on sex, drink, and movies. My terrifying descriptions of their debilitating effects were based on my fantasies about the tragic fate of Mrs. Lust. I began to realize that the world of Ottawa was divided into two camps: first came the civil servants and social workers who, by grace of their positions, were immune from the pestilences of desire; then, bringing up the rear, the great suffering mass of humanity.

To this latter region, in their way, were consigned Benny the budgie and Gilbert the guppy. Since Mrs. Lust's change of boyfriends, Benny had regrown the feathers on his wings, but his chest remained bare. My father attributed this improvement to his daily exercise regime. He began to let Benny out in the mornings, too. Once I had so much trouble getting him back into his cage that I was late for school. I ran the whole way, trying as I ran to invent some excuse more plausible than the truth, but when I arrived I found the whole school standing in the middle of the football field as the result of a surprise Fire Drill.

We also had Atomic Bomb Drills. Crouched on my knees, hands laced behind my neck to protect vital nerve centres, I would wonder if fish and birds might take over the world after the rest of us had been fried. Mrs. Lust's new boyfriend, whose name was Albert, liked to discuss these matters with me. Watching Gilbert flash back and forth in his tank, usually handicapped by fins half-chewed by the more aggressive of his playmates, we would talk about life after the tomb.

Albert, who was extremely short but entirely covered in muscles, was an albino. His bleached eyebrows and colourless skin gave him extra dignity, as though he had already died.

"The way I see it," Albert said, "a fresh start is never a bad thing. There's lots of land up north, anyway. Plenty of room for new cities."

Under Albert's pink-rimmed but gentle eye, Gilbert swam acrobatically. His bitten fins began to heal themselves and so, along with Benny's improvement, a whole new epoch of health and stability was launched. It seemed to my brother and myself that under Albert's benevolent influence a household once a concentration camp for pets had become a veritable paradise. My parents, however, were entirely unaware of this fundamental change in the nature of our universe. The only thing that my mother noticed was the lingering smell of Albert's cigarettes.

My parents' enormous reasoning powers were such that my brother and I had long ago discovered the maxim vital to survival: one slip and you're finished.

Early one afternoon, just as Albert and I were launched into a cosy debate about post-nuclear geography, my mother pulled a surprise raid.

"Hide in the cupboard!" I whispered urgently to Albert, as my mother raced up the stairs. She had been a hurdles champion in high school and social work had not diminished her ability to leap the most carefully constructed barriers. But Albert, true to his post-mortal wisdom, did not know the meaning of fear. Dropping his cigarette into the aquarium, he turned to face the music like a man. Meanwhile, falling in slow motion through the blue-dyed water, a cloud of grey-black ash. After a few minutes this first deadly burst was followed by amber particles of tobacco drifting down from the floating hulk of Albert's filterless cigarette.

As soon as Albert had disappeared, my mother sent myself and my brother to play outside. But instead of going into our yard we began to walk down the street. The budgie next door was sitting happily in the window, screeching "Bye-bye" through the plate glass at the top of its tiny lungs. Two houses down, Laurence Clapman, the Beethoven of our immediate vicinity, was bent over his piano, head shadowed by the electric chandelier his mother kept burning day and night, pounding out his scales with volcanic fervour. And across the street, Mrs. Gilstein was mowing her front lawn. Around her temples, Greek-goddess style, was wrapped the sweat-soaked bandana she wore in silent reproach to those neighbourhood boys, like myself and my brother, who refused to endure her curses for fifty cents an afternoon.

When we got to the corner we turned, without speaking, towards Seed's Billiard Hall. As we walked by the house of a girl called Stacia, I remembered that only a few months ago she and I had spent two hours together, sitting in the sun on the front steps of our school, discussing the trials of Mrs. Lust. Stacia was a year older than me, and with her sculpted nose and ice-blue eyes she was considered to have a woman's face already. As I told her about the change in boyfriends, she nodded with the sagacity of a girl who was going steady with a man who worked.

"I can't explain love to *you*," Stacia had said to me. Just as, I thought, Mrs. Lust had said that there was no hope of my being different from other men.

Outside Seed's Billiard Hall was the usual knot of talking men. For a moment my brother and I hesitated, but then we pushed our way through to the open door framed in a dark haze of cigarette smoke, and plunged into the forbidden world of sin and retribution.

There were three pool tables, one of which was surrounded by the entire senior football team. Along the wall ran a counter with Coke and Honeydew machines, and at the far end of the room were scattered a few arborite topped tables. Sitting at one was Albert. When he spotted us he leapt to his feet and gave us a muscular wave; as we approached we could see that Albert was talking to no stranger, but to Mrs. Lust's first boyfriend.

"This here is Tom, my brother," Albert said.

"Good day," Tom offered. "How you been keeping?"

"Bad day, today," Albert said. He raised his eyebrows and stuck out his tongue, which made him look like a clown in whiteface. Then he took a sip from his Coke, opened his windbreaker, and took out his cigarettes.

"Want a smoke?"

"No thanks," I said.

"Don't worry," Tom interjected. "No women allowed here." It was strange to hear his voice again, and to see his complete lack of embarrassment at having been exchanged for Albert.

My brother said, "Thank God," but his voice squeaked. He was ten years old. He took a cigarette and then so did I. Albert offered us a match and we sucked the smoke in expertly, having already spent several years practising on cigarettes stolen during our parents' New Year's parties.

"She's a tough one," Albert said. "You must be proud to have such a mother."

"Got to hand her that," Tom agreed.

"I thought she was set to kill me."

"Yeah," Tom said. "I wouldn't want to cross her again. When she caught us in the living room, she tried to yank the belt right out of my trousers." He laughed.

The mention of trousers reminded me of Mrs. Lust and I began to feel depressed.

"If I got you into trouble," Albert offered, "you can hide out at my place for a while." I wondered where Albert's place could possibly be. Certainly not on the street of four bedroom houses where we currently lived. No more likely in the three bedroom neighbourhood we had previously inhabited, or even in the two bedroom rental units where Mrs. Moulds had been our guardian. The only place I could imagine Albert living was in one of those rusted chrome trailers illegally parked down by the river.

"You missed something when she caught Tom," Albert said. Tom laughed and Albert leaned towards us. I had never seen Albert angry before; but now whatever my mother had given him to swallow was rising to the surface, turning his cheeks and forehead a delicate, albino pink. Even his colourless hair seemed to be flushing and rising bloodfilled from his head, and he began to look like an exotic tropical bird.

"What was he doing?" I asked Albert. Because, despite his anger, I felt it would be disloyal to speak directly to Tom.

"Hey," Tom said. He took me by the shoulders and turned me to face him. "We were only doing . . . what people do."

By the time my brother and I got home, Benny was on the drapes and my father was in the kitchen with my mother, helping her to prepare supper.

During the evening not a single word was said about Mrs. Lust, and so totally was the subject sealed over that I completely forgot about Gilbert and the cigarette butt until after dessert, when my father began chasing the budgie around the living room. In these chases I was always the helper, so that even though I had become obsessed with fear for Gilbert adrift among the tobacco leaves, I was forced to play my usual role.

This involved gently beating the drapes with a broom – Benny was increasingly ingenious in his abilities to hide among the folds – while my father made soft, pigeon-like noises to seduce him back to his cage. "Birds are like people," my father liked to say. "If you are reasonable to them, they will be reasonable to you."

Most of the time his philosophy seemed justified, at least with Benny, but on this particular evening Benny was upset, and no one could doubt that the cause was the terrible scene he had witnessed this afternoon. Flying nervously from drapes to bookcases to the framed French impressionist prints my parents collected, Benny became more agitated the more my father hummed and cooed and whistled sweetly.

Squawking, cheeping, and smashing his newly feathered wings as he bumped around the living room, Benny went on such a rampage of hysterical tension that my father stood up and boomed out, in the loud, deep voice he used only for disciplinary emergencies: *"Benny, go to your cage!"*

Benny responded by lurching off in a new and wild direction, this time landing on my mother's spectacles where, to his eternal sorrow, he lost control of his bodily functions.

My mother screamed.

"Benny!" my father roared. He grabbed the broom from me and with one powerful swipe sent Benny flying from one of our matching ceramic table lamps towards the wall. From there, my father explained later, Benny must have gone straight to budgie heaven. His body, meanwhile, remained in our living room. Crumpled on the floor, the fuzzy baby feathers of his wings folded pitifully over his bare chest, Benny lay in noble repose. Since his neck was not broken, my brother and I decided he must have died of a heart attack caused by my father's savage outburst. But our grief for Benny was softened by the knowledge that, in his last doomed moments, he had taken some kind of revenge on my mother for banishing his friend Albert.

It was decided that Benny's grave should be directly beneath the dining room window where he had spent so much of his life. The digging was quick, even fully-feathered he had never been large, but afterwards we stood looking down at the newly-turned earth telling the stories about Benny that had already become part of his legend. A whole hour passed before I was free to attend to Gilbert. Running up the stairs to my bedroom, I had already accepted the fact of his death. But when I pressed my nose against the glass, I was still shocked to see every one of his playmates floating belly-up on the surface of the water, bits of tobacco hanging like cigarettes from the corners of their lips.

Gilbert, however, was cavorting through the water in an acrobatic frenzy. Seeing me only inspired him further. With a sudden, dolphin-like burst of genius Gilbert zoomed straight for the sky, arrowed between two of the bodies of his former tormentors, and broke the surface of the water. Shooting at least six inches above it, he executed a perfect double flip with a twist and a half before landing, fins first, on the hollowed remains of Albert's fateful butt. From this platform, with virtually no pause, he soared into the air once more, this time contenting himself with a double-twist somersault into the depths of the water, where he commenced to swim with the lazy grace of an emperor surveying his newly-conquered domain. If only Albert were here, I thought. Maybe nuclear war wasn't so bad after all.

When I woke up the next morning, Gilbert was still swimming. Though obviously hungover, he was clearly the most triumphant kind of survivor. In fact he lived on for years, even after I left home. It wasn't until the summer of my third year of university that Gilbert began to fade.

By that time many things had changed. Mrs. Lust, after two more boyfriends, had been fired, never to be replaced. My mother's eyes had improved dramatically with age and she no longer wore spectacles. Onto the back of our house, projecting over the grave of Benny the budgie, a glassed-in summer porch had been added. The girl next door had unexpectedly become a mother and was living with a geologist in Tahiti.

The night Gilbert actually died, I wasn't even home. I was down at the river in a car with a girlfriend, doing the sorts of things that I had been warned against in Health class. When I came back to the house, near dawn, my parents were waiting for me in the living room, drinking coffee. They were dressed in dark suits and sunglasses, smoking cigarettes. My father had already shaved, and over her freshly washed black hair my mother wore a hat with a white veil.

Gilbert was lying where they had found him, at the bottom of the aquarium. He had died with his eyes open: still-youthful, fine brown eyes that in his final moment had frozen into an expression of infinite love and regret.

Sentimental Meetings

Planet and sky met in a long curved strip of light. Joseph Benares rubbed his eyes, straightened his neck, disengaged the elbow of his neighbour from the pocket it was trying to make between his ribs.

"*Bonjour, mesdames et messieurs . . .*"

The voice of the captain came through the overheated air in a broken cloud of static. When Joseph turned from the shining silver of the sea to look towards the front of the cabin, he saw the stewardess was already beginning to distribute trays of micro-wave heated buns to the sleeping passengers.

At nine-thirty he was in a taxi wheeling crazily through the traffic on the Rue de Rivoli. His suitcase had been the first off the baggage belt. Good luck? A token of appreciation for flying Air Canada? "Everything is worse than it was," the taxi driver complained. But the sky was blue and Paris sparkled as if it had just jumped, freshly-made, out of the tourist magazines.

When he locked the door of his room behind him, Joseph felt a brief moment of panic, the familiar nightmare of hotels falling like a blanket over the brilliant day. His hands began to shake, as if some new, unwanted neighbour had jostled him. He lit a cigarette, sat down on the bed, and focussed on the wallpaper. A wild tropical garden of violent yellows and greens leapt humidly from the wall.

Hands still trembling, he unpacked his suitcase. "Travel light," Tomas had told him, then laughed, his old man's voice breaking free in a sudden burst of life. "That way you can bring home souvenirs." Ironed shirts, two ties, a pair of formal shoes yet to be broken in, grey slacks, a sweater. Beneath his shirts was an address book. Printed in gold leaf on the cover, courtesy of a client: JOSEPH BENARES, BA, MD. On the blank pages were written the names his grandfather had given him. "These are your family," Tomas had pronounced, reserving for this statement the solemn tone of voice in which he annually predicted his death. "They belong to you. You belong to them."

Joseph went into the bathroom to splash water on his face. Black *spic* hair, parted in the middle and falling straight to his collar; olive skin stretched tight over high cheekbones; hazel eyes rimmed with red and surrounded by an increasingly defined network of lines and wrinkles. He was suddenly reminded of his first trip to Europe, more than fifteen years ago: then the face had been slightly thinner, the hair longer, the eyes red with drinking instead of reading.

The garden on the wall had subsided to a mild hum. Joseph went downstairs, where he handed in his key, then walked through the crowded streets until he was at the Jardin des Tuileries. On the airplane he had been thinking about Christopher Columbus: not the voyage to the New World, the sudden shock of the future. He had been trying to imagine the savages Columbus had brought to display to Ferdinand and Isabella. What had the poor kidnapped victims made of the glittering Spanish court? According to the books they had failed to be impressed – in fact, they had reacted to the cradle of civilization by growing sick and dying.

Joseph stopped at the entrance of the Jeu de Paume. Inside were real paintings, paintings immortalized ten million times on posters pasted across the walls of North America.

"*Monsieur, s'il vous plaît*, please!" In front of him was an old woman, dressed like Raggedy Anne. Joseph reached into his pocket, the unfamiliar French coins thick between his fingers.

"A family friend" was how Tomas had described her. She was the niece of a second cousin once-removed, a connection that would have been entirely meaningless had not Joseph instantly seen that despite her official distance she was only a slightly foreign model of his own exact family.

She answered the door and waved him in. About fifty years old; spiky salt-and-pepper curls; a silk dress carelessly worn over a body that might once have been beautiful but was now retreating to the wiry Benares frame; hazel eyes that were duplicates of his own. As she was taking his coat she suddenly turned and grasped his shoulders, kissed him on both cheeks.

Still not a word, and as he followed her into the apartment Joseph suddenly wondered if she was a mute. "She lives alone," Tomas had said, but without adding whether she had once been married, or if her aloneness was simply a disease – the same disease, perhaps, that Joseph had: thirty-seven years old and unmarried, all the Benares genes and chromosomes begging to be reproduced. There were no pictures of husband or children on the walls, so Joseph assumed that the "family friend" had also failed to multiply. But because she was a woman and past the age, her position was definitive: her supply of eggs – about four hundred, according to the textbooks – had all dropped into oblivion.

"English!" she suddenly burst out.
"English," Joseph repeated.
"You speak English," she said, in English. But her accent was disturbing.
"Yes."
"Do you speak a little French?"
"A little."
"I speak French," she said, still in English, and Joseph

realized that her accent had been borrowed from Greta Garbo. Her name was Hanna Santangel, but on the mailbox in the foyer it had been engraved Mme H. G. Santangel. Now Joseph felt like an awkward schoolboy faced with an exam he hadn't prepared for.

"*C'est un plaisir de –*" he began stiffly, but Hanna interrupted him before he could even pause to search for the right phrase, cut him off with a flow of English so voluble and sibilant that Joseph had no idea what she was saying. Then she was in his arms, weeping and sobbing and talking all at once. When she stepped back, reaching into her sleeve for a handkerchief, her face had been transformed from that of an elegant and impervious Parisian to that of a crying child.

"There were so *many* who were killed." She opened the drawer of the buffet which immediately spilled over with hundreds of photographs. Hanna grabbed them in handfuls, displaying them for a second then dropping them to the floor as she reached for more. "First Franco and then Hitler. Look." Joseph felt the tears streaming out of his own eyes; they had started without his noticing. And he was crying, not only in sympathy with this stranger's sudden outburst of emotion, not only out of sorrow for the other millions of strangers who had died, but for the whole jumbled parade of pictures, the universe forgotten, the cascades of family snapshots – carefully posed portraits, lovers holding hands or trying to look serious enough for a wedding; children crinkling their foreheads to make themselves look like bullfighters or movie stars – all of them with the Benares stamp, all of them in some strange way exactly alike, natives of the country of which Joseph had suddenly found himself a citizen.

It wasn't until late at night, when a bottle of wine had warmed them, then been followed, first by a pot of coffee to keep them awake, and then by cups of hot chocolate to help them keep cosy in the hours after midnight, that Hanna

Santangel brought out her oldest treasure, the will of her great-great-great-grandmother, a woman who had been born in a Jewish ghetto in Kiev more than two hundred years ago.

The will had been written on parchment, and the parchment itself was yellowed like the skin of a very old man. It was written in Hebrew, which he had learned to read as a child. Hanna made him pronounce the words aloud, only translating as he finished each sentence.

"You are not much of a Jew," she laughed. "You don't even know your own language." But then, as he blushed: "I was only joking. When they come to round us up, I promise you will be included."

She had shown him everything. Her tears, the photographs, the scrap of parchment that had evaded two centuries of destruction. Now she gathered up the evidence and put it away in the buffet drawers. As she bustled about, restoring the room to its original order, Joseph had the sudden feeling that they were becoming strangers again.

She turned to him. Joseph stood up, knowing it was time to leave.

"You must be exhausted," Hanna said, "listening to my rantings. I can't let you go back to the hotel like this, in the middle of the night."

"It's nothing."

"I insist. You didn't come all the way across the ocean to stay in a hotel."

When Joseph woke up he could hear the shower from the room next to him. By the time he got to the kitchen, Hanna was there, her short hair wound into tiny damp curls.

"You slept well?"

"I dreamt about the will."

Hanna smiled. "The will is nice to have seen, but I would like to offer you something more, something that is real. If you can spare me a little of your holiday . . . ."

At the hotel, the clerk looked at Joseph with a knowing smile. "You found a good restaurant last night?"

"I found an old friend."

Joseph saw the clerk's face suddenly freeze, then move into a question mark. He realized that in his fatigue he had forgotten to speak French, had spoken Spanish instead.

"Excuse me," said the clerk, "I thought you were an American."

"As a matter of–"

"Breakfast will be sent right away to your room, *señor, milles excuses.*"

In the bath Joseph looked down the surface of the steaming water to his protruding toes. "Feet tell the story," a landlady had once advised him.

On his right foot, his big toe was bent and mis-shapen. During an argument with his wife, his ex-wife, in fact, he had emphasized a certain point by kicking one of the heavy porcelain lamps her mother had provided as dowry towards the picture window in their living room. In the heat of his anger Joseph had wanted to drop-kick the lamp – or better, his wife – through the thermopane glass and onwards to a ten storey journey to the sidewalk below. Instead, the joint of his toe had cracked on impact. Joseph, too furious to go to the hospital, had bandaged it himself. When he finally did leave Judith, he was still limping, hardly able to carry his suitcases to the elevator where Judith, her eyes suitably swollen, waved goodbye.

Out of the bath, Joseph dressed himself in the white suit he had bought for the journey. He was short, wide-shouldered, the desire of his stocky, ex-soccer-player's body to run to fat only partly warded off by frequent, boring sessions in the university swimming pool. Today his eyes were darker. My emeralds, Judith used to call them, when the motor between them was well and purring. Olive pits, she would say, when it wasn't.

Having slept since his return from Hanna's, Joseph found himself ferociously hungry. Walking the back streets from his hotel towards Montmartre, he stopped beside a huge mounded display of fresh shellfish. He leaned over a basket of raw oysters until he was enveloped in their briny smell. Moments later he was inside the restaurant, a bottle of sparkling white wine and a platter of clams in front of him.

"Joseph Benares!"

Joseph's head jerked up. The voice, the face, gradually filled his mind like an unwanted image slowly coming into focus during a bad film.

"Mind if I sit down? Who would have thought to see a white man in this country?"

Norton Meredith's voice slipped out like an unnecessary sub-title. First Joseph had found himself remembering long-buried scenes with Judith; now here was one of the original supporting cast: Norton Meredith, best man at the wedding, court witness at its legal dissolution.

"Excuse me for not shaking hands," Joseph said. "They're covered with clam juice."

"For God's sake, Joseph, how *are* you? You look *great*."

"Thanks, Norton."

"I stopped drinking years ago, but I admire those who keep it up, despite everything. Go ahead, don't mind me."

Norton Meredith, Joseph slowly realized as the close-up of his face receded and his whole body became visible, had changed more than his drinking habits. He was wearing a black leather jacket, gleaming and supple, and about his neck was wound a white silk scarf. His hair, silver, was down to his shoulders, and when he shook his head with delight Joseph could see that he had gold earrings.

"I *moved* here. Got right out of the rat race. Never *felt* so good. Set up a practice treating homesick tourists. I *love* it here. What's *Judith* doing?"

"We're divorced."

"I *know* that. But don't you keep in touch? Even today,

it's more unusual to get divorced than to get married." Norton paused, then smiled, a gleaming display of ivory and gold.

"You look great," Joseph said. "You really do."

"I thought you'd *never* notice. I came out."

"That's wonderful."

"Not out of the *closet*, you fool, I'm not a faggot. I mean that I came out of my shell. I'm *myself* now, none of the old defences."

"Congratulations."

"You old cynic. Come to dinner tonight, meet my *maîtresse*, nothing special, she has lots of friends. Someone for you."

"I promised my aunt."

"Forget your aunt. Or bring her. You know, Joseph, since coming to Paris the old *fires* have heated up again. I can't get enough."

"That's wonderful."

"If you can't come tonight, how about tomorrow? I have a card, here—"

"Norton, I'd love to visit you. But I'm leaving Paris tomorrow. Maybe when I get back."

"Where are you going?"

"Spain, with my aunt, I promised—"

"Keep your promises," Norton Meredith said. "And don't worry about me. I'm in a clear spot now, I can come with you. Really, it's no problem." He stood up. "I'll meet you at the airport and, look Joseph, let's be straight. Do you still hold it against me? One night, she wanted comfort. That was all. You know what master Freud says, Joseph. Sometimes a cigar is just a cigar."

Both of the guards were elderly and fleshy, dressed in black uniforms that must have fit better when their muscles were younger. "*Guardia Civil*," Hanna spat out as they walked towards the synagogue. *Synagoga del Transito* it was listed in the guidebook, the most beautiful synagogue in Spain and the entire world.

The guards stood in front of the door, smoking and talking, and even as he mounted the steps Joseph could see that the ticket window was closed.

"The synagogue is not available today."

The guidebook explained that the synagogue had been built by Samuel Halevi during the fourteenth century. Earlier in the day they had gone to Halevi's palace, now a national monument. It was, the guidebook pointed out, entirely reconstructed on historical principles. Unlike his palace, Halevi had survived neither intact nor reconstructed. An over-zealous investigator had tortured him to death while trying to discover the hiding place of his supposedly fabulous riches.

"We would like to see inside the synagogue," Hanna said slowly, as if talking to an idiot.

"It is occupied today," replied the guard, turning away.

Hanna pushed past him into the lobby. Joseph followed. To the right was a door which had a sign proclaiming it a library of ancient Hebrew books and documents. It, too, was closed.

A van pulled up outside the synagogue, its muffler-less motor roaring in the heat. The doors opened, television cameras began to emerge.

"Look," Hanna said to Joseph, who was already looking.

The director was talking to the guards, all smiles, a letter was being shown. Joseph heard the guard say that yes, he had a difficult job. It was better to work guarding one of the great Cathedrals, the truly magnificent churches whose visitors understood the duties –

"They're German!" Hanna suddenly exclaimed.

She was right. The film crew were talking German among themselves as they dragged their cameras up the steps and into the doors of the synagogue which were now flung open.

"They're getting in," Hanna complained to the guard. "Why can't we? This is my nephew, a very important man, a doctor. He is all the way from America and I have brought him here, from Paris, to see the roots of his people."

"The synagogue is closed," the guard repeated. But now Norton Meredith had appeared from around the corner and was engaged in violent conversation with the film director. Taking his white scarf from his neck and waving it as he spoke, one hand on the director's shoulder, Norton led him towards the guard.

"These people are my guests," the director now said. "There has been a misunderstanding." He was blond, a Teutonic viking. He stepped between Joseph and Hanna, put his arms around them and ushered them inside the synagogue. "Bureaucrats," he said, switching to English now that they were inside. "They're the same in every country."

Within a few minutes floodlamps had been set up, the entire synagogue staked out by the crew. There were no prayer benches, no ark for the scrolls, no altar. The building was as bare as an empty warehouse. Five hundred years ago the synagogue had been turned into a church; more recently it had been restored as a tourist attraction.

" . . . a documentary on religious freedom," the director was explaining to Hanna. "I want to show that people are finally, after so much bloodshed, free to follow the god of their choice."

"There is only one God," Hanna muttered. "And people don't choose Him, He chooses them."

"That is your opinion," the director said with a smile. The sounds of camera motors filled the room; electric whirrings that buzzed about like gigantic moths, the floodlights trailing their course.

"We wanted to film people praying," the director said.

"Heart to heart is the most effective, one person to another."

"No one prays here."

"So I was told. I tried to find a Rabbi in Toledo, but he was unavailable."

"You should have been here six hundred years ago. There were dozens of Rabbis then."

The director smiled. "The Jewish community has become very secretive. Believe me, I understand these things. During the war – "

"You are a very intelligent man."

"Between intelligent people it is possible to discuss these things, to put the past behind us."

They were staying in a hotel that had been converted from the palace of a Cardinal. The doors of the hotel were reinforced with steel flanges, the windows barred. "Look at these," Hanna said to Norton, pointing to the door and the bars, "these show how much the people loved their Cardinals."

"Love must go both ways," Norton replied. "Believe me, I know."

There was a new, honeyed note in Norton's voice, a professional tone that he must have learned to use on his homesick tourists, and as Joseph winced he saw Hanna draw back as if she had been buzzed by an unpleasant insect.

In his room, Joseph splashed water on his face and hands, looked up at his face in the mirror. "You can't pass a mirror without staring at it," Judith had once said angrily when, in the middle of a fight, he had been frozen by the expression of his own contorted anger in the living room mirror.

That was the last fight, the one that had ended with him packing his books and clothes into one of Tomas' gigantic leather travelling bags. Perhaps that was the very night Norton had been summoned for help. Perhaps that was even the night when Norton, until then an awkward psychiatric resident with the breaking voice of an adolescent, had learned to speak in smooth and reassuring words.

But no matter how hard he tried, Joseph was never able to remember Judith's face. Even now, missing her for the first time in years, he was unable to summon more than her green-brown eyes and the peculiarly tufted hairs that grew at the centre of her eyebrows.

At the actual moment of the divorce, long after the final separation, Joseph had looked across the room at Judith, wondering if some unexpected and cosmic reconciliation might still take place. While other couples parted, she had come to sit beside him, leaning her shoulder into his chest for comfort the way she used to, bending her mouth to his so that he would hear her whispers. "How have you been? You look good. Norton tells me you gave a wonderful lecture last month." And he had whispered back, whispers as close as kisses, saying that he was fine, that Norton was still an asshole, that she was looking more beautiful than ever, that she must have gone south to get such a winter tan.

Afterwards they had gone to the courthouse coffeeshop, the three of them. When Norton excused himself Judith had leaned over to Joseph and said that she still loved him: maybe they should go back to her place – one last time to make the ending happy.

Now Norton had made another tactical disappearance, and Joseph was alone in the hotel dining room with Hanna. After coming back from the synagogue she had been so angry that lunch, served in the immaculately white dining room, had made her violently ill. But she had returned to the table and the wine. "A friend of the family, a real guardian angel." Joseph again remembered Tomas' description. "A saint."

"Look at them," Hanna gestured, pointing to the busloads of tourists who were enjoying their meals without getting sick. "Even these pigs do not want to put their past behind them."

"You're feeling angry," Joseph said soothingly, as if Hanna was a patient to be babied. "Try to let yourself relax."

"Relax!" Hanna sputtered. But she ordered a cigar from the waiter, who delivered it to her without comment. Soon the odour of cigar smoke filled the room and, calmed, Hanna ordered a bottle of Calvados to be brought to their table.

By four o'clock the dining room was almost empty. So was the bottle. Hanna was on her fourth cigar and had already explained to Joseph how the Castilian kings, beginning with the massacre of the Jews in Toledo in 1391, had taken over one hundred years to climax their drive to rid Spain of its Muslim rulers. "In 1492, the reconquest was finished. Ferdinand and Isabella were on the throne and for the first time in eight hundred years Spain was ruled by Spaniards – and Christians. To celebrate they expelled all the remaining Jews and sent Columbus off to discover the New World."

"What about the Inquisition?"

Hanna's voice dropped to a tone so low and bitter Joseph could barely hear her words. "I don't have to tell you what *that* was like. To amuse the population the priests organized gigantic acts of faith – in which Jews were tied to the stake and burned. These often took place in the sites of the old Roman Circus, where the Romans tortured the Christians. And yet, if you speak to a medieval scholar about such things, he will tell you that the medieval mind knew nothing of the concept of irony."

In the far corner of the room a new party was being seated: it was the television director and his crew. Beside the director, and talking loudly in a strange mixture of German and English, was Norton Meredith. In the course of the afternoon he had changed into a white silk suit. With his silvery hair and bright scarlet cravat he looked like an overpriced gigolo.

Before Joseph could deflect her attention, Hanna had spotted them. "Pigs," she said, in a voice that carried across the empty room. The director stood and bowed to her. On Hanna's pale cheeks now appeared two round red discs, like makeup carelessly applied by her anger and the Calvados.

"I met those types during the war. Do you have them at home?"

Joseph shook his head. Home? He could hardly remember it. Even the airplane trip from Toronto to Paris was a dream fast receding. The waiter was arriving with a bottle of champagne on a tray. Two glasses. "Compliments of an admirer," he said to Hanna. Hanna leaned across the table and kissed Joseph on the lips. She tasted like cigars, but her lips were soft and sweet just the same.

"Cheers," Hanna said. "That was very kind of you."

"It wasn't –"

"Don't tell me. I don't want to know. Anyway, the fool ordered French champagne. Spanish is better."

Two glasses into the champagne, Joseph felt his head come miraculously clear. He ordered a package of cigarettes and a second bottle of champagne, this time Spanish. He also requested that a new box of cigars be brought to the table.

"No more champagne," Hanna directed, "without brandy to accompany it. Otherwise the bubbles make me dizzy."

Joseph discovered that it no longer mattered whether his eyes were open or shut. Either way he was presented with a roseate haze of which Hanna was the out-of-focus centre. The new champagne was brought, uncorked, consumed. As they drank, Hanna was telling him about her war experiences. Terrible nightmares. Moments of comfort. "Imagine that," she said over and over again, urging him to the full horror. But despite his best efforts he was unable even to remember what she had just described, let alone imagine it.

"Terrible."

"I've never met an American who could drink so much."

"I'm not an American. I'm Canadian."

"There's a difference," Hanna said, "but I keep forgetting what it is."

They were standing up, and suddenly Joseph realized that her compliment was deserved. He wasn't drunk at all. In fact the whole room pulsed with a brilliant clarity that was more real than ordinary reality, even more sober than ordinary sobriety. As he straightened his back and stretched, Joseph felt such a burst of well-being and confidence that he lent poor Hanna his arm. She stood on tiptoe and Joseph seemed to imagine that she was still talking to him. "Before Tomas left Spain he brought me from Madrid to Toledo for a week, to see a specialist for a rare disease I had contracted. My disease, a consuming desire to be drowned in the arms of Tomas Benares, went away soon enough. In the meantime he showed me the city of our ancestors." Before Joseph could even imagine his dwarfed and aged grandfather with this strange woman, Hanna started forward and Joseph, arm linked with hers, began to stride out of the dining room.

"Good evening."

Joseph turned, sensing a vague half-wanted familiarity. Then Norton Meredith spoke again. Words of extraordinary brilliance began to form themselves in Joseph's mouth. Then he pitched face forward across the heavily laden table of the director.

"A nice dive." The director's voice was only inches from his ear. "Daring and full of spontaneity. Truly, my friend, today you are showing us the best side of America."

"Head first, too," Hanna added. "That showed a lot of style for someone who travels with only two shirts. Frankly, I admire the courage of such a gesture."

The cells of Joseph's mind felt suddenly invaded, and

what had been so brilliantly clear was entirely fogged over. The director and Norton Meredith had lifted him into the air, carried him like a dead man to his hotel room, and slid him, clothes and all, down the cold porcelain of his bathtub. Then they left the room while Hanna removed his clothes and turned on the water. Now he was naked in the steaming bath, modestly covered by a thick layer of the rosy bubblebath Hanna had so thoughtfully provided.

"Are you sore?"

"Sore?" Joseph squeezed his eyes closed and sent an inquiring scout beneath the surface of the water. After a few moments it reported that sensation had completely disappeared from his bones and his muscles.

"You are feeling no pain," Joseph said.

"*I* am feeling no pain," Hanna corrected.

"Could I have a cigarette?"

Hanna wiped his face with a towel, put a cigarette between his lips, lit it for him.

Joseph felt his lips make contact with the filter, a sharp sensation as the smoke filled his lungs. As he exhaled he noticed that he was beginning to see again, though the room was still smudged. He put a hand to his glasses, lifted them off. One lense, the rose-coloured one, was covered with an uneven layer of tomato sauce. The other was curtained in what might have been coffee with double cream. He dipped his glasses in the water, drew them out again. Save for a slight mist, the bathroom snapped into focus. But Hanna's scarlet and the rosy happiness of her bubblebath survived intact.

Now the director and Norton Meredith came into the room. The director approached Hanna first, leaned over and kissed her neck. Hanna jerked back, but not too quickly.

"Don't mind me," the director said, "I'm off duty." He sat on the edge of the tub, brandy glass in hand. "Is this your first trip outside of America?"

"I'm not American, I'm – "

"He's a Jew," Hanna interrupted. "Jews are international."

"That's it," Norton exclaimed. "A man who travels discovers *himself*."

"Of course," agreed the director. He leaned over the tub, his muscular arm stretching across the water until his long white fingers came to rest on Joseph's naked chest. "Welcome home."

A Love for the Infinite

If words have lost their meaning, why not look for meaning in silence? – Octavio Paz

He is lying on his back.

His skin is cold, his feet are beginning to go clammy in the thick, insulated boots, and his hands are clenched to themselves. But he can feel the warmth of the golden-pear sky flowing through him, and as he senses this special warmth in his blood he begins to match the steady rhythm of his heart to the slower beat of the changing season.

His head is cradled in dead golden leaves. Crisp and yellow they curl around the tendrils of his hair, poke their waxy corners into the warm, secret creases of his ears.

Soon it is not only his heart that is contracting and expanding, but the whole earth that is pulsing with it. And as he is lying on his back and looking into the splintered yellow rooms of the sky, he feels the solid thumping of his heart coming, not from himself, but from thousands of miles under the ground, each beat starting at the absolute centre of the planet.

He closes his eyes and the sun only shines brighter.

He sees himself lying on the yellowed poplar leaves, the hot gold truth of the sun exploding inside him, leaking gently from his eyes and ears and nose, gold waxy truth leaking out of him until finally he is covered in it, a softly ossified gold wax dummy lying on the autumn ground, soaking up the last October sun.

He woke up and it was night. The sky was deep black, dotted with billions of carelessly burning stars. He wiped the gold from his eyes, dug it out from his nose and ears, unstopped his mouth.

He stood up, brushing grass and leaves from his clothes. He was conscious of the drug, now. He stretched, trying to make his bones go into place. He could feel where they had been bent out of shape by muscles tense and twisted; by years spent hunched over a desk; by the steel-springed exercizers he used to flex as a boy, trying to develop shoulders in the places where his older brother's sweater crumpled in on itself.

Now he was older than Michael was then, older even than Michael had been when he died. What if he, too, had died? There had been a time, earlier in the day, when he was afraid that the drug might kill him; that the same demon that had snatched away Michael might have gotten to him, too, made him take an overdose, miscalculate the strength of his body. There had been a period of fighting the fear, and then he had finally given in to it. But it hadn't mattered; he had collapsed onto the ground and been drawn into the yellow leaves by a power that was indifferent to his fear, to his dead older brother, even to himself.

He pushed his fingers through his hair. Stretched, and stamped his feet on the ground. The night air was cool and beautiful. He could feel it blowing through him, caressing his skin and then passing right through it, refreshing his compromised bones, his exhausted muscles, the canals that faithfully carried his faithful blood.

He began walking down the hill and through the scattered trees that would take him to the trail. In the afternoon he had thought he was lost, that he was dying and lost, but now the landscape was utterly familiar, every curve and canyon of the rough ground known.

When he hit the old logging road his boots scuffed in the gravel. *This is the life*, he said to himself. *What I should really do is live here. I should build a fire to keep me warm, and in the morning start cutting down trees to make myself a cabin.*

At this thought he stopped beside a poplar. Through its black night leaves he could see thick rivers of stars. He slapped the trunk with his open hand. The bark was smooth and cold against his palm, and the leaves hissed. With both hands he grasped the trunk and tried to shake it. The tree stood firm. Finally, his whole body involved, he got the poplar slowly waving back and forth, its upper branches moving in faster counter rhythms, the leaves twisting and turning in the cold air.

Then he stopped.

The papery whisper of the leaves gradually died away, and he could hear the wind again breathing through the trees.

An hour later he was in his car, listening to the happy murmur of the tires as they carried him south.

He was standing up.

In the mirror he saw a reflection of himself: a thin, middle-aged man, his hands awkwardly twisted as he knotted his tie.

"We need ice. And did you feed the dog? We need more tonic water, too; you'll have to make a trip to the store." His wife's voice.

"I'll just finish here." His voice.

At the store, the 7-11 Convenience Store, everything was lined up in neat little rows. It *was* convenient, he told himself; it truly *was* convenient. Outside, he fed quarters into a machine and was scarcely able to believe his luck when a plastic bag of ice cubes came tumbling out.

It was only as he was walking to his car, one arm wrapped around a bag filled with cans of dog food and tonic water, the other carrying the plastic ice-bag, that he noticed it was snowing. A flake fell in his eye and melted there; the sudden sensation of snow melting into water, the warm water running down his cheek, reminded him of when he was lying in the leaves and his eyes ran gold.

City lights diffused in the skeined snow clouds. No stars showed. He sat in the car and remembered how it was to be driving when the drug was still running through him and he could feel the motor meshing in his brain, could somehow match up the pumping pistons and exploding cylinders with the memories of grade eleven physics and the time he and Michael stuck four giant firecrackers up the exhaust pipe of his uncle's rusted pickup truck and blew its muffler right through the back wall of the woodshed.

By the time he got home the snow had already stopped. And in his absence the first guests had arrived. Soon, he found himself almost drunk. Then, in a long unnoticed leap, the party had narrowed down to a little corner of the living room where a woman was insistently telling him something.

"I really understand you," she was saying. "God knows, you're not an easy man to read, you know what I mean, in your case you have to read between the lines and to tell the truth I used to wonder if there was anything there–" she laughed at her own joke, because he wasn't going to, and leaned closer "–but there it is, you've got something but you just don't want to let go." Her name was Mary, Mary McCallum right now, but it used to be Mary Samuels and before that it was something else, and before that something else again. This Mary-whoever was once his older brother's wife–"I owe it all to you," Michael's suicide note had read–and she had left him to marry the next in line. On that night Michael, in a manner that did not bear thinking about, had terminated his own existence. Ducked the donkey, kicked the bucket, blown his brains to Kalamazoo.

"What you've got," Mary was saying, "what you've got is what Michael never had, God bless him, though he ate his guts out for it, you know that? He did. Because you've got soul, dear ex-brother-in-law, dear honest-to-God 100 per cent polyunsaturated soul, forgive me, but you're too fucking timid to show it to anyone. You know what I mean?"

She had him pushed against the wall of his own living room, and the truth was that, although he was partly concentrating on what she was saying, he was also thinking that it was awfully unfair to be delivered this drunken, obscene lecture by the multi-married Mary right in his very own living room, pressed against the plaster he himself had so very carefully painted only one summer ago. One coat of primer and two coats of white.

"Well?" she asked. "Don't you have anything to say for yourself?"

"You're a great old-fashioned woman, Mary. You really know how to make a man feel important."

She laughed. "Don't be shy, now. Tell me what you really think. You *know* you're good, don't you, you just *know* it."

"No. As a matter of fact I don't."

"You kill me," Mary said. "Did I ever tell you that? You really kill me." She leaned closer. "I'll sell your house for you," she said. "You know what? I make more money selling a house than you do from one of your lousy little books. I mean you can *read* them, younger brother, but you can't live in them." She laughed again. "Sorry. I'm pretty funny tonight."

He was enclosed by the sleeping house.

Wearing his bathrobe, smoking a last cigarette, he walked around the downstairs, picking up stray ashtrays and glasses that had somehow missed the first round of cleaning-up. As he walked he listened, from old habit, to the sounds of the motors switching on and off.

Michael had taught him about the motors, about the

secret animals that made them go. The furnace, for example; he claimed the furnace was powered by the same Chinese moth who had built the Great Wall. This he had discovered when he found an empty green-tea box on the basement floor beside the oil tank. The refrigerator, on the other hand, was kept cool by the efforts of a thousand guppies who swam endlessly, breeding and reproducing in the freezer compartment.

There were two children, and when he had finished listening to the motors he listened for the sounds of their breathing. He had developed, when they were younger, the habit of waking up in the middle of the night to be sure they were still alive; and although he prided himself on being cured, he still spent part of every late-night wander in the hall, standing with his arms folded across his chest, listening for their breathing, and hearing with it the breathing of his wife, deeper and stronger, laid beneath the children like a deep, secure carpet.

Michael had taught him that, too: the listening. When they were children he and Michael had shared a room, and they had a special game. On certain nights, by pre-arrangement or surprise, he would wake up very late and Michael would be gone. In the delicious and terrifying secrecy of the dark, their parents asleep while they, the children, were totally awake, he would creep about the house looking for Michael. "You have to promise," Michael would say, "you have to promise to find me. Will you?"

"Yes."

Solemnly they would shake hands on it, agreed: their secret pact.

And then finally, when to giggles and terror Michael was discovered behind some huge and bear-like piece of furniture, they would prowl around the house together, using stolen matches to light their way. Until they found the kitchen – where they would open the refrigerator and, dazzled by the welcome of its sudden yellow light, steal bits of food to carry back to their beds.

When he had started taking the drug he had tried to conjure Michael up, had tried to convince himself that somewhere out in the God-knows-what ether and spirit world Michael was still findable, still hidden away in some corner waiting to be discovered.

There were the sounds of his family's breathing. There were the sounds of the motors. It was ridiculous to have machines heating and cooling different parts of the house; his life, he thought, would be so much simpler if he could take his Chinese moth north with him to the place where the leaves fell gold and waxy and the earth thumped in time to the beating of his heart.

His own footsteps were silent.

He moved through the halls carefully, bare feet sinking into the carpet, a ghost in his own house.

Upstairs the breathing sounds grew thicker. His children, who shared a room the way he and Michael once had, seemed almost to be choking, and, as he crept inside to kneel between their beds, he had the sudden sense of interfering with their dreams.

The oldest – his name was Michael after his brother – turned swiftly in his sleep, pursued or pursuing it was impossible to tell. And then, as if it were the most natural thing in the world, his eyes opened.

When his son's eyes closed, he knelt down and kissed his forehead. Then, to the sound of the motors and the breathing, he walked slowly down the carpeted stairs, through the kitchen to the basement. There he found his outdoor clothes and, after very slowly putting them on, he let himself out the side door into the driveway where the car was parked.

The snow started slowly, the flakes gently floating to the windshield where they immediately melted. But then, as the city was first one, then two hours behind, the pace picked up; and by the time he had turned off the main highway onto the twisting maze of roads that led to the old logging trail, the first snow of the season had become a small blizzard; and what should have been a bright morning sun was only a diffuse yellow presence.

At first he stayed in the car, unwilling to go out into the storm. With the motor running and the air warm and stuffy he had drifted into a series of dozing sleeps, interrupted only by brief moments of looking out into the grey curtain of snow. And then finally, groggy and stiff, he wrapped himself up and forced his way out of the car.

He was dressed almost entirely in his brother's clothes – because it was only after Michael had died that he began to share what had been his interests – and in some gruesome act of respect, superstition, or just morbid remembrance, he had decided to disguise himself as Michael on these trips north. Around his face he had even wrapped his brother's old scarf, a musty plaid flannel.

He was dressed as Michael, he was remembering him. But this time there was no drug to warm him, no chemical inner sun to guide him safely through the weather.

He breathed in the cold air and it was like a slap to his insides. Only a few days ago the sun had run warm and waxy in the poplar leaves; but now most of the leaves were on the ground, covered with snow. The few that remained on the trees were dark and brittle, like sour old men determined to outwait the coming winter.

He was lying in the snow.

The car was hours and miles away.

Michael had killed himself. So what? Was he obliged to follow him?

He was wearing Michael's warmest coat, a sheepskin coat with woolly lining and a huge collar that he had turned up to protect his ears; and as he lay in the snow, trying to feel the frozen ground gradually work its way through to freezing him, he was asking himself why Michael's death preyed on him so.

After all, he had not neglected Michael while he was still alive. Responding to an endless litany of late-night telephone calls and dense, scrambled letters, he had continually been the one to rescue Michael – from hospital beds, unpaid charge cards and parking tickets, mistresses who had outlived his short attention span, two drug overdoses that might have been botched suicides.

"You should try to straighten out," he once said to Michael.

"Why?"

"You're ruining your life."

"You live the life. You've got a career, a family, a book to write. You live the life and I'll do the fringe things, take the chances."

"For Christ's sake, Michael, you've got the same life I do – career, talent; you're the one with the talent, the boy genius. Your wife – "

"Mary? Oh, no, mister, that's no wife, that's a . . . I don't know." Michael laughed, the way he did when it was supposed to be a joke but it was really just a little shout of pain that he couldn't keep down. He was silent for a few moments. That was after the sleeping pill overdose, and he was in bed, his own bed at home.

"You could try again with someone else, Michael. Trust someone. Just because with Mary – "

"Just because," Michael repeated sarcastically. "No, it's not just because of Mary. Nothing is just because of anything." And then he smiled, that sudden, sweet, boy's smile that told you he had only been hiding, it had only been an elaborate joke with a sweet forgiving smile at the end. "You know what Baudelaire said?" Michael asked. "He said that the attraction of drugs is a sign of our love for the infinite. How do you feel about the infinite?"

The infinite was making him cold.

He stood up and brushed his clothes clean. He took his hands out of Michael's sheepskin gloves and slapped them together, rubbed vigorously against his nose, trying to make it feel something.

Then he stood without moving, facing north. North must be where Michael was. The wind blew up briefly, whistling sardonically in his face, like one of Michael's fake laughs.

"Michael," he shouted. "Michael, where are you?"

Then he turned his back on the wind. It was hours since he had left the car, and the land which had been so known to him only a few days ago now seemed utterly unfamiliar. After a few minutes the wind started again, pursuing him from every direction. With his eyes closed against the hurt of the cold he let his feet make the search for the old logging trail that would take him back to the car. Near the end, when he realized what might happen, he began to run. He didn't know what time it was, but the grey sky had taken on the faintest tinge of pink, as if to announce that the storm was over.

In the spring, they found him.

Wolves had torn apart the sheepskin coat, and the plaid scarf was wrapped around a nearby poplar. But the skeleton, surprisingly, was intact.

The car door was open and a month of rain had rusted the key into the ignition; it looked like a metal hand waiting for someone to shake it.

At the Empress Hotel

The bathroom light turned the skin of the maestro yellow, as if it had already been made into a lampshade. He brought the water in handfuls to his eyes, splashed it onto his hair and neck. His eyes, grey-blue, were now heavily lidded, but in his boy's face they had stood out like protuberant jewels.

He bared his teeth. Most of them were still there, polished and drilled, scraped white by the dentists. When he closed his eyes lights and pinwheels sparked across the insides of his lids, making them twitch and jump in company. He closed them tighter and massaged them with his fists.

The telephone buzzed at him. He went to get it, then stopped. It buzzed again. The glow of streetlights filled the room. He kicked off his shoes and lay down on his bed.

Vast webs of nerves stretched through his body, layer on layer, growing thick in his spine, knotting into a fist at the base of his skull, running through his brain in masses of red shot silk. The old lady's home-made brandy, so sweet going down, now boiled in his stomach.

Before they left she had cornered him in the kitchen.

"Are you happy?" Her eyes were pink at the edges and watered. She had gotten her hands around one of his arms. Her own arms were barely human, held together by old veins and scars, the thick silver bracelets she had somehow brought with her.

"I don't know," he said. He was lying. "I'm sorry," he said. "I am happy. It's a good life." He started to smile insincerely at her, and then found that the smile got out of control, his face split open with his sudden revelation. He put his arm around the old woman and hugged her. She smelled of powdered flowers. Then he stepped away, suddenly afraid of breaking her. And even as they all shuffled around the door, making their confused exit, she kept crying.

"Look at you," the old man had muttered disgustedly. "You're all sentimental fools. You give war a bad name." And then he had offered them his hand, still big-boned and sinewy.

The maestro tried to sink deeper into his bed. There were ridges and lumps in the mattress. Even with Marika to soften them he had woken up with a sore back. He caught himself listening for her footsteps in the hall. The old man was right, he *was* getting sentimental. Sometime soon he would begin to reassess his life; all the lost opportunities would present themselves and accuse him of . . . what? He was sure he could hear her in the hall. All the way home in the taxi she had slouched against the window, pouting as if he was supposed to feel sorry for her. An unnervingly familiar smell was beginning to penetrate the room. His telephone started to buzz again, its orange light flashing simultaneously. He ignored it. The smell made him hungry for cinnamon toast. No, that wasn't it. The old man would never have gotten involved with someone like Marika. The smell grew stronger. It was intensely familiar. A picture of a bomb began to form itself in his mind. As he rolled off the bed, the explosion came.

"You've been avoiding me lately," Marika said. She switched on the bedside light. "I tried to get through to you but your telephone must have been off the hook."

Only the lock was blown out of the door. Neat, she had always been neat.

Somehow Marika had gotten into the bed, and now the maestro was standing naked in the centre of the room. All these decades of wearing pants had rubbed the hair right off his legs. They looked unhealthily shiny, broken only by the red circles where the nylon socks had constricted his circulation.

"You don't even listen to me anymore. You used to love to hear me talk. You remember how we used to read to each other? You used to be so romantic."

"I'm not your husband."

Marika looked distressed and hid her face in her hands. All the years of glycerine had injured her eyes; now she could weep only for the cameras. While she wasn't looking, he slid into bed. She turned away from him. He burrowed under the covers and began to kiss her back apologetically. His kisses only made her curl up tightly, as if she had decided to turn into a snail. The maestro started to feel depressed. She didn't seem to understand how old he was getting, how difficult it was for him to wriggle around like this. He put his hand consolingly around the base of her neck.

"I hate being a woman," Marika said. When she slept, old complaints fell out of her. Despite everything her dreams composed her face, smoothed it out and filled the small hollows where the skin had begun to collapse. In the morning she always woke looking like a child, her cheeks round and innocent, only gradually taking shape as the day progressed.

"If it weren't for my parents, I wouldn't care."

"It will get worse," the maestro predicted. "At first you will feel terribly sad. You'll groan and moan that your beauty and ambition have gone. But instead of being ruined you'll find yourself perfectly content. All your old movies will suddenly be translated into Japanese. With your fabulous new wealth you'll buy a mobile home and travel around the continent, picking up strays and promising to be their grandmother. They will be insanely loyal and grateful. One day, when you are living in a village and walking down the road with a sack of turnips over your shoulder, you'll know that you have stopped hating yourself."

"And you?" Marika asked. "What will happen to you?" She sat up, crossed her legs, and lit a new cigarette with the lighter he had given her. He tried to imagine himself in the store, buying it. Now he remembered presenting the lighter to someone else, thirty years ago. In those days he had been truly romantic.

"I see you in the future," Marika said. "You move to a city, a city like this. At first you are starving. In order to make a few dollars you deliver handbills from door to door. The war has started again. One cold winter day you slip on the icy steps of a large stone house. A young girl dressed in blue cotton comes out to help you to your feet. She invites you into the house and gives you a cup of hot tea. In return you perform a tune on the cello which you have noticed under the coat-tree in the hall. The girl's mother appears from upstairs. She is the president of the local symphony association and your playing moves her to tears. It evokes images of her dead husband but she refuses to fall in love with you. Instead, she commissions you to give lessons to her daughter. In honour of her husband's memory she deeds you a small cottage with a brick wall around its garden. You procure a mistress who says she is your second cousin. She lives in the house with you and helps you furnish it in oriental rugs and sticks of incense. Occasionally you request that she dress in blue. She begins to bear your children and on your birthday you go into the nursery and play with them."

For the first time the maestro noticed that the hair on his belly and chest had turned grey. Only yesterday he had been pink and smooth.

"I have to admit," the maestro said. "Sometimes I start to get tired of you. When your husband needs you, I am no longer jealous. In fact, I praise your virtues to him all the time. Sometimes in the morning I would rather wake up alone."

"I guess this is the end," Marika said.

"I guess it is," the maestro admitted. "But what would we do without each other?" He laughed. "What would we do without each other?" he repeated. He turned to Marika. She had wrapped the sheet around her shoulders. In her hand she was holding a small gun, its tiny muzzle pointed directly at his belly. He reached for his underwear.

"Don't move."

"I refuse to die naked." Without looking at her he drew on his clothes: shirt, underwear, pants, socks, and laceless shoes. Then he sat down in the armchair the hotel had provided. She was beginning to make him nervous. His hands shook and his palms were sweating. His feet were sweating too; already they had soaked through the socks and had grown icy cold. "Throw me a cigarette," he asked. His voice remained steady for his irregular request.

"All right." The gun went off, a loud red blast. The maestro's heart expanded into a huge bird, furiously beating and clawing to escape his ribs. Then it cramped. He clutched at his chest, tearing at himself. The next thing he knew Marika was lying on top of him, kissing him passionately and sobbing.

Late that night, with Marika long asleep, the maestro found himself in the lobby of the hotel. Velvet-covered chairs lay emptily scattered about the tattered carpets. The chandeliers glowed a soft old amber, waiting for morning. Even the night clerk was asleep, his head resting on the counter, hopefully cradled in his arms. The yellow air was heavy and stale with the long hours of darkness. An umbrella of smoke hung over the arched room, and rising from the floor was the debris of the thousands of words and bodies that had poured over it. Like an old, frozen tableau the brass spittoons posed at random, overflowing with butts and candy wrappers.

In this silence the maestro could hear the memory of whistles and applause. He imagined himself on stage once more, his body smelling of soap and perfume, his hair thick and slicked back to curl about his ears, his coat stiff with recent pressing. Like the conductors who had once conducted him, he raised his arms. Out of the corner of his eye he saw a package of cigars lying unopened in an ashtray.

Once he had carried a small gold knife to slice the tips from expensive cigars. Now he used his teeth. He scratched his upper lip and remembered when he and his brother had grown moustaches. *There are times when a man needs a moustache.* The maestro considered this. He observed himself sitting in a faded velvet chair, smoking someone else's cigar, searching the various truths of life and waiting for his to arrive. He had his feet up, and gratefully his blood ebbed away from his swollen ankles and flattened arches. His time for a moustache had come before; somehow, it might come again. He exhaled twin streams that blossomed at the edges of his vision, then closed his eyes.

Perhaps a moustache would not be so bad. He rubbed his hand over his face and with his eyes still closed he turned his head towards the piano. In the afternoon he had come down to this same lobby, played Mozart sonatas, and provided other entertainment while the management served their famous tea. *Yes*, he said to himself, *a musician can never starve.* He raised his eyelids slowly. The night clerk had woken up and was standing in front of the piano, polishing the keys with extreme care.

"You see?" the doctor had said. Shooting his cuffs and spreading his big scrubbed hands in the air. On one wrist the doctor wore a watch with a leather band, on the other a bracelet advising that he was a diabetic. The maestro tried to place the exact date of the interview. It had been two years ago, almost precisely; the same afternoon he had seen Marika for the first time, on a movie screen.

"I interview many men like yourself," the doctor continued. "You come in the door guiltily, afraid that you might be sick after all. Sometimes your wife or your insurance agent has sent you, sometimes you make the appointment yourself, picking the name out of the phonebook. You say you have been feeling tired. It is hard to get up in the morning. You can't be bothered making love to your wife."

The maestro nodded. He had wasted his time. The doctor probed his mouth and his bowels. Looking thoughtful he hammered on his ribs and listened to his lungs and heart. With a small flashlight he looked into the maestro's eyes, and with a steel hammer he tapped his knees until they swung. There had been only one new moment. Standing in the office, with the eyes of the doctor and the nurse upon him, he had bent over to begin dressing again. For one second he had seen himself: his legs now thin and crooked, his belly rounded with flesh and hair, his shoulders bent forward. Then everything had become familiar as his thick arms swung into view, the veins popping out as his fingers gathered his pants, pulled them up, and put everything out of sight, like a curtain covering a stage that had been improperly set.

"What you need," the doctor concluded, "is some sort of excitement. Come back to see me if you strain yourself."

The maestro went home. He took off his shoes and sat down on one of his precious oriental carpets. He spread out the book the doctor had given him and tried to do the exercises that it showed. Against his bare back the wool was itchy and rough. His hip scraped along the centre of a Japanese Garden. When his stomach was sore, and his back and legs were stiff and aching, he gave up and went across the street to the movies.

In the second reel he saw her. She was playing the wife of a famous explorer. While he sailed off to sea, while he experienced unendurable privations and fulfilled himself in dazzling triumphs, she stayed at home and wept. To console herself she fell in love with a sailmaker. They spent long, enigmatic evenings standing on the coastal bluffs, wildly staring into the western stars, watching the sword of Orion rise inscrutably over them as the morning advanced. Her face on the screen was dark, and in a mean, tight way almost beautiful. From certain angles her beauty blurred and she looked like a strange and dangerous ferret. Meanwhile her husband's cause suffered its reverses. He was sent down from his post as governor of the island he himself had discovered. Then the new governor threw him in chains and ordered him home. Marika appeared again as he stepped off the boat, his hands and feet shackled together.

"Are you home in disgrace?" Later he found out she considered the unnecessary question the highest form of elegance.

"Aah yes," the husband admitted. "I am home in disgrace." This was to be the anti-climax of the story. The camera centred in on him. The fiery red hair of his youth had bleached white with fatigue and worry. His features were ruined. His eyes burned only with defeat.

"I have nothing left," he said. His voice poured onto the audience like gravel onto cement. "Only your love remains to me." His pitiful eyes opened to her.

Marika's narrow face filled up the screen. Her dark skin smouldered over her high, aristocratic cheekbones. There was a shadow moving across the background. This was her lover. For one long, barely subliminal moment her skin seemed to twitch. An unmistakable message was telegraphed to the audience: Who am I? What am I doing here? "Then do not despair," she finally said, "we will be together still." The movie ended. Only the addicts were in tears.

The maestro went out to the lobby. There she was, standing by the cigarette machine, holding a small box of popcorn. No one else recognized her.

"Excuse me . . ."

"Yes?"

He looked down at her feet. He saw she was wearing her shining black boots. For some reason the interviews always mentioned her boots. He tried to remember other things he had read about her. Unfortunately the entertainment pages all ran together in his mind; all that was left was an image of Marika and her husband climbing out of a taxi in front of an expensive nightclub in New York.

"I couldn't help admiring your performance."

"It was not outstanding," she said. She looked at him without interest. Even her popcorn was unopened.

"It was unusual," the maestro insisted. "Not everyone would have been able to appreciate it." At this he thought she was beginning to smile. He was reminded of her face when she first encountered the sailmaker. "I admire a woman who can be honest," the maestro said. "It is so rare, today." He let a slight trace of his accent show. Perhaps she would recognize that they had something in common. The fluid Spanish consonants were already sounding in his mind.

"Too many people are honest," Marika replied. "Promise you will only tell me lies."

Customers were beginning to come in for the next show. He realized she was waiting for his signal. They left the theatre and stood in the afternoon sunlight of the street.

"If you would not be insulted . . ." the maestro began. He stopped. She was scuffing her feet impatiently, and she followed him across the road in that same nervous, hurried way until they were mounting the stairs of his apartment.

"Will your wife be home?"

"I'm not married." He unlocked the door and led her inside. On the living room carpet he saw the doctor's exercise book. He picked it up and put it on the mantel, beside a poorly fashioned bust of Socrates.

"I live a quiet life," he said, putting on a record. Now he saw that her nervousness had transformed itself to the same bored expression she had worn while standing in the harbour watching her husband's ship return. He looked down at his wrist to check the time. His watch was gone. He wondered where he had left it. Marika was sitting in his one chair. Her boredom was now becoming an irritation, and she was swinging her foot back and forth.

The maestro stood casually by the mantel. "I was going to get another chair," he said. "You can't find anything decent here." Then he paused before adding, as if it were of no consequence, "I lost all my furniture in the war."

"Oh, yes," Marika repeated absently, "the war." She smiled in forgiveness, the gold-rimmed teeth flashing in one more code.

He found a bottle of sherry and two glasses. Soon they were on the floor, kneeling in front of each other. In her eyes he could see the reflection of the dusty city windows, the plant he had hung from the ceiling to remind himself of something.

"What would you say . . ." he began. Without his watch his wrist was naked and inoffensive, hardly worth looking at. In a public school basement six miles away children were waiting for him to come and teach them how to play Beethoven. Soon they would ask him to teach the opera. And he would teach them, too, all the sleek young children, fat and well-kept like prize animals for the breeding, he would line them up and teach them to sing Wagner.

"You don't mind?" she asked. Her face was almost touching his. She must have been much younger when the movie was made. The sun illuminated the channels between her hairs, lit up the surfaces of her skin so he could see the faint reminders of her youth: old freckles, sunburns that had long since faded, layers of lives that had been melted into a uniform colour by quartz lamps and the southern sun.

"It doesn't matter," Marika finally said. Then she walked out, her black boots slapping down the stairs.

"You are so kind." The maestro looked out the window and watched her disappear down the street. He took his book of exercises from the mantel and lay down with it on the floor. The sherry was making everything impossible. He drank from the bottle until even the sweet taste was gone.

Later that night, she came back. "What about your husband?" the maestro asked. On her wedding finger Marika wore a lumpy diamond ring.

"He won't let me in," she replied. "We had a fight about his mother." They lay down on the maestro's rented wooden bed. They took off their clothes. When it finally happened, he felt as if a long-buried splinter was being torn out of him, cutting everything open again. He fell asleep immediately, hoping she would be gone in the morning. In his dreams he had already moved to another city.

The next day made the hotel lobby new once more. Light from the snowy afternoon lay across the audience in long, lemon sheets. They sat in apparent peace, their chairs accompanied by small stands of tea and biscuits, their hands and laps busy with newspapers and magazines. The most refined stared delicately out the high, latticed windows; others simply smoked and glared expectantly at the elevator.

They were not disappointed. At exactly four o'clock the maestro appeared. He stood momentarily beside the piano. No one noticed the slight shadow of his new moustache. With one thumb hooked into his watch-chain he dispensed the necessary seconds. "Good afternoon, ladies and gentlemen." The heads of the audience now swung to meet the lady advancing across the lobby. Wearing a white lace shawl she came straight through and without a single bow sat down at the piano. "Permit me to introduce my colleague," said the maestro, "the famous Marika. And now, as I promised, the story of my escape is continued."

As he stepped forward, Marika obliged him with an introductory chord.

"You will recall that circumstances had forced me out of the mouth of the cave. Still within were the couple who had saved my life. Even as I tried to decipher the uniforms of the soldiers who were beginning to surround me, I wondered if this couple, old enough to be my parents, had protected me only because I reminded them of their own lost child."

The maestro was delivering his speech to an empty chair in the middle of the audience. He looked around at Marika. She was leaning against the piano. He looked out the high, narrow windows that lined one wall of the lobby. Giant potted palms hung from the ceiling. A waiter silently wheeled a silver cart about the room, weaving among the impassive listeners, refilling cups and providing samples of the cook's latest and most elaborate pastry.

"They marched me along the trail and up to the top of the cliff. From there we could see over the whole river valley. Cannon and anti-aircraft guns were being set up to establish the position and, a few hundred yards back on the plateau, tents were being erected. It was in the midst of these that I was led to the commander.

"He was as they had described him: a puny man supporting a head shaped like a giant, rounded egg – almost completely bald, only a few wisps of light-brown hair about his pale ears and temples. He was sitting behind a huge desk in a chair especially raised to support him.

" 'Your brother told us to expect you.' He opened a desk drawer and took out a small leather pouch.

"For some reason I was offended by the way the commander's white hands held my brother's last effects.

" 'Soon the war will be over,' the commander said.

"In the most distant corners could be heard the insistent humming of enemy bombers and, behind their motors, the fighter escort, a shrill, high-pitched buzz.

" 'Only men who are afraid to die make good soldiers,' the commander said. He took out a small suitcase, placed it gently in the centre of his desk and unlatched the brass catches. He opened it slowly and ceremoniously. It was his makeup kit. With great care he cleaned his face and applied a new foundation. With a thick pencil he traced the outline of his eyes. Then he bent forward and powdered his scalp. While the commander flossed his sharp, white teeth, an aide brushed off his coat and drew a steel comb through the few remaining hairs: they wound out of the crown of his skull like underdeveloped ferns.

" 'Discipline,' pronounced the commander. 'Discipline is the key.' Bombs were falling all around us. The aide brought out a bottle and three brandy glasses.

" 'Long live the King,' shouted the aide.

"The commander swallowed his brandy.

" 'Long live the Empire,' he replied."

In his hands the maestro now balanced the pouch that had belonged to his brother. Time had turned the leather soft and supple, darkened it with the sweat of his hands and pockets so it fit into his palms like his own skin. The maestro held the bag out high for all to see. Then he turned it upside down, emptied it out, and threw the contents at his benevolent listeners: loaves and fishes, teeth and rings.

He looked out at the audience, letting himself see them as they shifted into focus. The afternoon had stripped their flesh away. Now they were only skeletons, their bones shining and streaked with blood. In a strange ballet they all rose from their seats, stretching their stick arms and clasping their hands together, clacking sounds of metal and bone. And then, like strange, bony flowers they began to float about the room, clustering in small groups, talking and gesturing in their small, hollow voices. Marika took his arm; her white lace shawl flowed from her shoulders like a wedding gown.

They passed through the crowd and out the hotel lobby onto the street. Fat cars hurled by, throwing up snow and slush. They walked about the square until they found shelter beneath the awning of a jewellery store. Through the thick window the maestro could see rows of cheap diamond rings. Just as the jeweller himself appeared, his hands filled with velvet-lined boxes, a taxi drew up and quickly Marika and the maestro climbed inside. The driver's head was shaven close, the picture on the back seat told of his decorations.
"The usual?"
"Of course."
The taxi wheeled into a narrow cobblestone alley and began to crawl through it, twisting and turning to avoid the battered garbage cans and cartons of refuse. Marika searched out a package of cigarettes from her purse. With his eyes closed the maestro could still see the crowd dancing in the lobby, their bones flailing through the smoky air. When the taxi finally came to a stop they were out in the suburbs, not far from the edge of the city.
Standing on the steps of a small, neat house was the couple who had saved the maestro's life. They were wearing thick coats and fur boots, all covered with a powdery layer of snow, as if they had been waiting for hours.
"It's still the same," Marika said.
The old woman smiled. "Nothing has changed."
They were in the living room. An oppressive grey winter light fell across the satin couch, the long walnut dining table.
One corner of the room was dominated by an old-fashioned gramophone. On top of it was a picture of the commander, a studio photograph that surrounded his great,

fragile, bird's head with a soft halo. From the kitchen came the smell of boiling vegetables, and of chicken and veal frying in deep pans of their own fat. With great ceremony, the old lady walked about the room turning on the lamps, as if this was the one occasion when night would be denied.

"This is my brandy," the old lady was saying. She produced a crystal decanter for them to admire. Glasses appeared. The maestro touched his to his lips, tipped it back; the brandy burned like acid on his tongue.

The old lady smiled. She was wearing a dress that hung loosely about her bones, unsure of where it was supposed to fold. "We read about you in the paper all the time," she said. "And we always go to your movies."

"Acting," Marika said scornfully. "Anyone with a pretty face can act." It was true. She was growing old. Her face would soon be bony and mean. "I want to write the story of my life. My agent is arranging it."

The old man nodded vigorously. He started to speak, but his mouth was full of *hors d'oeuvres*.

"He gets so excited," the old lady said. "Many people would like to read about you."

"It's true," Marika admitted. "Everyone knows I am an expert at falling in love. It's like a disease. As soon as one romance begins to fade, I find myself drawn to another. Of course, I would rather stay with the first. For a week or two I even remember the good times that we had, the way I would wake up in the morning feeling warm and full, bubbling with life at the sight of my beloved. But then, when that memory goes, I look at this man whose grubby and bristly body is lying there, more likely than not stinking of sleep and alcohol, and I ask myself: Marika, what are you doing in this zoo? And what can I say? Nothing. The attraction to the new person becomes longing, soon the longing is deep yearning. I throw myself helplessly at his feet. He cannot resist such perfect love."

"He can't?" the old man croaked. He had accepted one of

the maestro's cigars and was doubled up with silent coughs. His wife turned to him and he hastily hid the cigar behind his back.

"But he does," Marika continued. "Perhaps he even fails to see me. Or he tells me of his wives and families, of the thousands of humans and animals and old-age pensioners that await his personal attention. Sometimes he won't even talk to me. He just sits and stares morosely out the window. That's the worst. Seeing him so dejected and depressed, brought almost to suicide by my own worthless adoration, I am filled with sympathy and passion. I offer to leave at any moment. I begin to bake bread. I demand that he come to New Zealand with me. I describe my painless death with true enthusiasm. He cannot resist such perfect harmony.

"He feels sorry for me and decides to prove that he's human. So he tells me that he feels love too. He begins to boast of the bony loneliness of his soul, the tearing anguish of his nights. Soon his tears are staining the carpet.

"At this point, I begin to hesitate. I am afraid that my mild infatuation may begin to deepen."

"But it never does," the old lady murmured.

"No," admitted Marika, "it is never brought to a finish."

The maestro found himself blowing tactless smoke rings. He had never once thought that the commander might be photogenic.

"Perhaps I am cursed," Marika suggested. "In the end it is always a clear, starry night. We go outside. It is spring. You know how the night smell of spring is unbearable. For a long time we are unable to talk. Quietly he begins to tell me his ambitions. His ambitions are born in the cradle, where he discovers he is an orphan. All through his terrifying childhood he watches his mother slave to keep this small, struggling household which exists solely in the hope of his father's return. Long after the last moment, years and years past the time he might have been useful, the father comes limping home, weak and old, Ulysses on his last legs. The son, who has grown bitter and joyless, helps him in the door. At the first available opportunity he steals the old man's watch and leaves. In his heart he knows he can discover better worlds than this."

The old lady glanced sternly at her husband. He had discovered new continents of brandy. "Don't worry about me," he whispered.

"He wants you to continue," the old lady interpreted. "He knows of whom you speak." The maestro had a great desire to disappear into his expensive clothes. Instead he began to make long and intricate calculations. Series of algebraic equations flashed through his mind. He deduced that the odds were only mediocre that his cigar would outlast her explanations.

"When the orphan decides to run away it is the middle of the night. For a few moments he is content to walk about the house in silence, listening to the disgusting sounds of the old father snoring, the long, hopeless sighs of the mother who has been almost faithful. Then he himself begins his travels. After countless adventures and hardships he asks himself what he is searching for. For weeks, perhaps months, he stumbles about, letting the question seethe in his innocent mind. Finally, he realizes that he has discovered the nature of his own true quest. Like his father before him, he is Ulysses. His destiny courses through his blood with great, urgent certainty. All that remains is the most trifling of details: he needs someone to wait for him so that when it is over and he has sacrificed his youth, there will be something to come home to.

"The next morning he takes a bath and begins to search for a likely candidate. He wanders through the streets and the countryside in a happy trance, overcome by his own romantic love. After days, weeks, months, he finally finds her. She is sitting at a table in an outdoor *café*. By her mysterious manner he knows she is a shepherdess from a nearby hill sent to town to buy supplies. In moments he is beside her, making his plea. Only when he has courted her for years does he realize she wishes he would apprentice himself to a shoemaker and make some money so they could settle down. Before he can even tell her of his wonderful dream they begin to fight and bicker like a couple of grandparents. Finally she refuses to see him and he, heartbroken, wanders off to another city.

"Again and again he is unhappy in romance. At times he thinks there will never be any solution to his life, that he might as well drown himself and forget it. But even in the worst adversity there is a mysterious force that keeps him going. One day, a cloudy day that has been sad from morning to night, he realizes what it is: his own ineffable sorrow. Finally he has something to fall in love with. After a few happy weeks he becomes pregnant with it. Months pass. He begins to grow lines on his face. His voice drops. He leaves his beard untrimmed. At the suitable moment he gives birth to himself and emerges, shining and sad, in such depths of despair that he is very briefly human."

Marika emptied her glass and poured another. Her mouth was stained with wine and cherry brandy. The maestro realized that he had never seen her drunk. This was a new role, one which would have begun only if the movie continued past her husband's homecoming. He tried again to remember when he had first loved her. Though she still wore the shawl, it seemed to show more than it concealed, suggesting thousands of tiny movements and details behind each word.

"For a few weeks he happily floats in this serene interval. He goes to movies, he reads books, he remembers his childhood. He recalls the vast ambitions he once had, the great intuitive flashes of his destiny as Ulysses. Though he is bitter and ironic about his failure, he is almost able to forgive himself: his sadness makes up for everything. And at this very instant that almost comes to pass, my life crosses with his. It is arranged by chance. A friend of a relative invites me over to dinner to meet her nephew. There is not much to be said for him."

The old lady nodded knowingly. "Yes, yes," her husband croaked. With his arm extended to its entire surprising length, he accepted a new cigar from the maestro.

"Even before the evening arrived I began to fall in love with his pitiable state. By the time I arrived at the house I was shaking with anxiety. But the moment I actually saw him, all my fears fell away. He was magnificent." Marika looked apologetically at the maestro. "Of course you did not know him then. Circumstances had reduced him to little more than a skeleton. Though he spent all day exercising and combing his hair in front of a mirror, the truth is he was as weak as a rabbit and going bald besides. He sat at the table like an adolescent, hardly able to manage his knife and fork. Yet I could see there was something noble in him, something that only needed to be encouraged. After dinner we were left alone. We sat right here—" Marika patted the empty seat of the couch beside her. "And he told me the story of his life. It took only a few embarrassing minutes."

The maestro felt himself beginning to sink. What a depressing tableau they must have made: the vampire and her over-age victim. Yet no doubt the old lady had found the circumstances overwhelmingly romantic. After rushing through supper she had feigned exhaustion and, in the convenient absence of her husband, snuck upstairs to lie on the floor of her bedroom, ear to the boards, picking up each nuance of their predictable chatter. Naturally, in this stage play which even the actors could hardly have believed, there were more silences than words. Perhaps, with the lights dimmed, under the pressure of fatigue, Marika—ten years younger—might almost have seemed soft and romantic. Even before morning threatened to interrupt she must have thrown herself at him; though now she would probably tell lies about the purity of their love.

"If you ask me," the old man suddenly croaked, "it

stinks." He waved his cigar defiantly and tapped the ash on the rug. "What of it? It's my rug. Don't interrupt. You don't suppose I haven't felt sorry for this poor boy?" He pointed his cigar at the maestro. "Yes, *him*. Who cares about her stupid husband. *This* is the boy she should have married. What a life they could have had together. A real life." For the first time the maestro noticed that the old man had been growing smaller every year. His carefully striped white shirt billowed out from his hollow chest. The collar was too big, and even the black bowtie he affected no longer disguised the way his neck had become brown and scrawny. "Don't look at me," the old man said. He turned to Marika and shook his head despairingly. "You idiot."

Marika said nothing. The blood rushed to the surface of her skin. Her hands, her arms, her throat and face, even her legs turned the deepest of reds, as red as the cherry brandy she was pouring into her glass. "You're no good for anything," the old man pronounced. "I'm going to call a taxi." He pulled himself up from his chair and staggered out of the room.

Wearing his striped trousers and his undershirt, the maestro stood in front of his mirror and shaved. His cheeks, chin and throat were joined in long, continuous curves. The razor found no resistance as it swept through the stubble and soap, leaving little islands of speckled white foam in the sink each time it was tapped clean.

"Are you awake?"

"Of course." Marika had placed a cup of steaming coffee on the counter before him. With one finger he wiped his lips clean. He held the coffee to his mouth. Its steam clouded the mirror, heated the soap on his moustache and made it run down into his mouth. He put down the coffee and took up his razor again. It was then that he remembered.

"What is taking you so long?"

"I almost shaved my moustache."

"You don't have a moustache."

"Ah, yes," the maestro said. At times he could not help admiring her. He put his tongue in his cheek and poked it out to ready it for the razor. In a moment it was clean. He lifted his chin and shaved the soap from his throat.

"My husband was asking about you," Marika said. "He would like you to join us for dinner this evening. We are also entertaining the assistant manager of the hotel, the local skydiving champion, and two chambermaids."

"You are irresistibly famous," the maestro replied. He splashed his face with water and inspected the final result. His moustache was barely visible. Twisting his neck, he could regard himself in profile. From this angle its shadow was darker. *There are times when a man must go into disguise.*

"You're jealous, again. You always get like this when you're jealous. If you knew yourself better you could spare us both."

The maestro came out of the bathroom. Marika had spread a clean white shirt for him on the bed. The hotel laundry had starched it so stiffly that he had to force the buttons through their holes. He worked the collar with his hands, trying to soften it for his neck. Marika held up his jacket for him. Then he stepped into his newly polished shoes.

"Your tie is still in my room," Marika said.

He put the key into his pocket, and they went out into the corridor. As always, it was empty. They walked slowly down the faded carpet. In this hotel, which was almost old, the windows in the halls were made of stained glass.

Before entering her room Marika crossed herself and muttered something under her breath. The curtains were drawn and the light was dry and quiet, like a magazine that has been preserved in a suitcase. In the midst of the room stood Marika's brocaded false wall. Littered about were bits and pieces of various costumes. He found his tie on a hook in the bathroom. The towels were all fallen down, pushed in a damp heap against one wall. He stood in front of the mirror, identical to his own, and began to work the tie under his collar. He made the final adjustments slowly, deriving a strange comfort from the familiar black silk.

When he stepped out from the bathroom, Marika was sitting dejectedly at her dressing table, her elbows on its glass surface, her head cupped in her hands. The maestro helped himself to cognac.

"It's no good," Marika said, "I can't keep living this way." She was wearing a long velvet skirt and a white lace shawl. She shrugged her shoulders hopelessly and pulled the shawl more tightly around herself.

"What way?"

Marika looked at him. He could feel her eyes searching for his, trying to grasp their centre. In the movie she had looked this way, too: the first night with the sailmaker, when they were about to make love; and later, when the explorer came back and she was about to resume her inert life with him.

"You always try to tempt me," she said. She smiled. Her mood had changed. She got up and went to stand beside him. In her high, polished boots she was almost as tall as he. But he felt infinitely bigger. He took her wrists in his hands. The bones were narrow and fragile as chickens' bones, so close and fine they threatened to break under the passive weight of his fingers. He released his grip and slid his hands down to enclose her thighs. They were amazingly warm, supple and alive, swimming still with secret plans.

"Do you love me?" she asked. She played nervously with his silk tie, and the lines about her eyes dug in deeper.

"Of course," the maestro said absently. "I live for nothing else."

"So," said the night clerk. "You're growing a moustache."

The maestro rubbed his hand over his upper lip.

"She'll leave you, anyway," the night clerk said. "You know she will."

The maestro nodded. He was looking at the night clerk's face. Long and narrow, with grey pouches under the eyes, his face seemed to have slid from boyhood into middle age in this one long winter.

"I loved a woman once," the night clerk offered. "Not my mother, I mean."

He stood up to lean against the counter. He was staring across at the maestro who now turned his chair towards him and, in recognition of this conversation, bit the tip from a new cigar.

"She used to come and meet me here," the night clerk said, "when the place was deserted like this."

The night clerk's voice was dry and hollow. The maestro stripped it of its words and let the nasal sound reverberate through him. When he was young he had learned to listen to music this way, to let his whole body be the sounding board.

And then, as the night clerk's disappointment faded, the maestro let his eyes take a slow census of the lobby. Once again it overflowed with the garbage of the late night hours; and the maestro, looking at the confusion of twisted chairs, ashtrays that needed cleaning, crumpled-up remains of the day's papers, turned his head slowly, carefully scanning every last and faded moment. It was like opening a book and sinking into a print so fine, a catalogue of detail so exhausting, that finally he was lost in a tide of tiny living fragments. He began to feel dizzy and sick to his stomach. Inside his clothes he was shrinking: his skin was shrinking away from the old cloth that carried the memory of a thousand nervous hours; his nipples were trying to escape the shirt that had rubbed against his chest for decades; even his neck had gone suddenly taut, trying to leap out of the collar that ringed it.

He forced himself up out of his chair. He could feel the heat rushing to his face.

"She's waiting for you," the night clerk said.

But the maestro only saw the night clerk rising to meet him, his body lifting up behind the counter, arms outstretched, a gigantic, wretched bat.

The maestro screamed.

The night clerk leapt over the counter and into the main lobby, old photographs leaking from his pockets as he bent over the fallen musician.

"No," the maestro whispered, "no." He struggled up from the floor, his hands firmly clutched around the night clerk's neck. The river of the other's life rushed through him; and the night clerk gagged and gasped. The maestro discovered that, as he pressed his thumbs against the bristly Adam's apple, the clerk's eyes began to bulge and his tongue inched out of his mouth, turning him into a reluctant, purple-faced doll.

"Don't you dare," whispered the maestro. "Don't you dare."

When the clerk was finally still the maestro stood up, quite calm, and walked over to the piano where he stroked his moustache and began to play.

"Love," the night clerk narrated, "it leads you into places dark and scary. Into corners weird and wary. Just like Joseph and – " He looked towards the maestro and a peaceful light suffused his face.

"I wouldn't have thought so," the maestro said. "No, I wouldn't."

There was a long silence and then as the maestro's music continued, grey skeletons of the night drifted in and the seats began to fill.

Café Le Dog

Let us say it is April in Paris, which means that the sun is rising early and strong, more than enough to burn the skull out, so if you are still dizzy and pie-eyed from the night before, there are worse places to have your coffee than Café Le Dog. I won't say exactly where it is, just to be difficult, but if you happen to be near Boulevard Raspail, perhaps only a few steps from the Montmartre cemetery, then you might stumble upon this place.

The name of the owner is Gaston Fournay. He comes to sit and talk with me now, though he didn't used to. He's got a face made up of little cushions: round, puffed cheeks, drooping jowls, an underjaw like a bullfrog's. Don't ask me how he shaves. I've never put the question to him, either.

I said pie-eyed in the morning, and since I am no ordinary drunk – or if I am I don't want to know – the implication is that the night was filled with wonderful poetic visions. But before we dive into the bitterness of art, the lot of the poet in this century of shit and machines, let's just forget it.

On the other hand, like all cynics, I was once an idealist. In my teenage years, for example, I played football and read poetry. And when I came to Paris I was still full of literary dreams. The first thing I did was to rush over to my uncle's place, a publishing house specializing in police novels and under-the-counter pornography. He was in his office. I had to stand outside the door while he completed his telephone conversation. Even with my flawed French, it was easy to understand that he was having an argument with his mistress. Then I was let into his office. He was the exact opposite of my mother: fat instead of thin; darkly hairy instead of pale and refined. He was wearing a hat, and his office smelled of French cigarettes.

"You're the boy," he said. "What do you want?"

Last night was pretty bad. It started here in the afternoon pleasantly enough. I had a couple of beers with Gaston's sister, Marie, and then we decided to go for a walk along the Seine and maybe celebrate Friday night at a cheap seafood restaurant where they know us.

Don't get the wrong idea. Marie and I are old friends but not romantic. That is to say we see in each other derelicts who can never be revived, but we are willing to give each other a little human comfort, if you know what I mean, but not too often. Anyway, you get the picture: vagabonds of indeterminate sex toppling towards a common destiny, but still sufficiently dignified to resist a mass grave. Or maybe it would be enough to admit that I can look her in the eyes, but only when we are in a public place. Have you ever noticed that you can tell true love because the smell of the truly beloved never offends? The fact is, I admit it, I could go on like this forever. But I've learned not to.

Why am I still in Paris, you probably want to know? To see me, you would know right away that I am a foreigner. What betrays are the British tweed jackets that I always wear. At first I wore them because, living in one cheap hotel after another, I had a tremendous fear of losing my passport. Fifty times an hour I would pat my pocket to be sure it was still there. Then I moved to the room where I still live, a room not so far from Café Le Dog, and I hid my passport under the floorboard. That made me feel like a real Frenchman, but I kept wearing the tweed jacket anyway, because

I had gotten used to its protection. Besides, I am a tourist at heart, in the worst way. Not for seeing sights – I'm such a snob that I've never even *been* to the Louvre – or experiencing strange places: the truth is that I am one of those people who always feels more comfortable in someone else's house, someone else's life, someone else's dreams and beliefs.... Why go on? You get the idea – I'm addicted to explaining things until my explanations fall inside themselves and begin to mumble and stagger about drunkenly, searching for a graceful exit.

I came to Paris in desperation and my uncle gave me a job in his publishing house. But after a few years he died and his company went bankrupt. Meanwhile, my bad poetry had appeared: three embarrassing little volumes that I buy up from bookstores and destroy whenever I have some spare cash.

"A poet," people used to say, admiringly, when I was introduced at parties. I learned that a woman who accepts you as a poet also accepts your basest desires. At first I was flattered. I thought it was my genius they admired. Then I realized that they didn't care who I was, what they really admired was the spectacle of themselves risking venereal disease for the chance to spend a night disguised as a Muse.

"Maybe you will write a poem about me," they would often say the next morning. Sometimes I did, even while they were eating breakfast. But they never wanted to read it – and when they did they were always disappointed. I don't blame them. Basically, I am like other poets in one way at least: I hate everyone. The portraits, therefore, were never too flattering.

Don't mistake me. I don't think that I am some truth-seeker while the rest of humanity walks around in blinders. What bullshit that is. If I am a poet – which I am not – it is only because I am socially maladjusted in a poetic direction. I am also socially maladjusted in other directions, but as a neurosis, poetry offers a career.

To this aspect of my existence Marie is indifferent. Thank God. With her I feel like a real person. A total asshole, but without pretensions. To put it even more bluntly, if possible, Marie and I have an understanding: we understand that we are both losers in the game of life, that we never even knew what the game of life was, that somehow we ended up middle-aged and ugly and completely unnecessary, but that's life so we might as well enjoy it.

Maybe I am being unfair here to Marie. Just as she is indifferent to my poetry, perhaps there are things about her which I have missed. Naturally I can't remember, but I will say that I think Marie is basically a good person. Let me go further. When the rest of us are sweating in Hell, Marie will probably be in Heaven. Firstly, because she is a woman – despite everything you hear about them, most are probably goody-goodies on their way to a higher reward – and secondly, because she has already suffered enough, why torture her further?

To return to something I hinted at: Marie is smelly. That she wears too many clothes and they trap her sweat is probably the reason – but more important is Marie's fundamental desire to repel. Unlike Gaston she has a very nice face, though it has been wrecked for daylight by her daily two bottles of wine, and even her figure is not bad. Of course she was once quite beautiful: she has shown me pictures of herself when she was employed by various gentlemen as a part-time wife. In those years she probably spent hours a day in the bath, powdering, scraping and perfuming herself. I wish I could have met her in that era, when I still carried my verses in the pocket which used to hold my passport. But then Marie lost her looks. "I just sagged one day," she explains it. She still receives a pension, others would call it blackmail, and at night we often walk by the luxurious house of her last lover and current benefactor. Once we even saw him: driving a German car he wheeled into his steel-doored garage. Marie ran for fear he would think she was snooping but I lingered. Out of the garage came a well-dressed businessman, you know the type – British suit, square, jutting jaw, close-cropped hair, piercing eyes. He looked about sixty. His wife was covered in furs but sulking. Unlike myself, Marie is a real Parisian. Her family has been here for generations, a long, uninterrupted string of cheap courtesans, nuns, and small shopkeepers. If I were Arletty I would make a movie of her life story; if I were still a poet I would write verses to her courage. But what does poetry have to say about steel reinforced businessmen? Even in French such a line would be hard to swallow.

Meanwhile it is morning at Café Le Dog. The dog in question is a real one; his name is Claude and he is lying underneath my table with his white head resting on my feet. Claude is named after my alter ego and worst enemy. But, take love where you can get it, as the old song goes. This morning I feel deeply empty, almost poetically so, or perhaps what I am feeling is not emptiness but sadness. I am drinking brandy with my coffee, to thicken the blood, Gaston says.

In front of me is a letter from my mother. It came two weeks ago. *Dear Camille*, it begins. Of course Camille is not my name. If it were, I would be even more depressed than I am. Nonetheless, Camille is what my father called me on his dying day. I was seven years old; the death took place in my father's bed; everything was arranged in the best of taste despite the fact that it was a rush job. He was sitting propped up by two pillows, and my mother had dressed him in his silk pyjamas. She was not yet thirty; he was much older but his illness was sudden and unexpected. A heart attack. It happened while I was at school, and by the time I got home his fate was already settled. "Camille," he said to me, his voice had a fine French horn timbre polished by decades of Cuban rum and cigars, "take care of your mother."

Those were his last words, and to this day no one knows why he called me Camille instead of Jacob, which is my real name, or even James, which is my middle name and was my father's first name.

I am planning to visit you later this spring, when the flowers have established themselves and the pollen season is over. Your apartment sounds magnificent. How marvellous it must be to wake every morning to a view of the Seine. I have often imagined you writing your poetry while gazing at its famous waters. Do you really have twin black maids? My life here is so boring in comparison. But I have spent the whole winter taking French lessons from Mme Dufresne so now I have only my wardrobe left to worry about.

Don't jump to the conclusion that I have lied to my own mother, although I have, but not the specifics mentioned above. Firstly, the letters I send to my mother are composed not by me but by Marie, whose knowledge of English was gained by reading the entire *oeuvre* of Henry James, twice, in the American edition. She sends letters to my mother that are never less than twenty pages long, and sometimes she forgets to show them to me. Secondly, my mother lives in a nursing home for the mentally disturbed in Montreal. She shares a room with the above-mentioned Mme Dufresne, and over the years they have not only taught one another English and French, but have taken correspondence courses in Hungarian, Polish, and medieval Latin.

Next month this entire block is being torn down for a new apartment building, and the doctor has said I am cured. I have made a reservation to leave on my sixty-fifth birthday, and after that I may never see my country again. To think that for years I have been in the land of the unstable and now I am to become an expatriate in another way. But if life is not one journey after another, Camille, what is it? Now that I am getting ready to set out on my travels, everything that came before seems insignificant. Already

I feel as if I have become, in my modest way, part of the scintillating group you have described so generously in your letters. Does Jean-Paul Sartre really ask after me at your Friday night soirées? I have read all of his works that the library here at the home has, and there are dozens of questions I am dying to ask him.

Everyone seems busy: that is the attraction of Paris. Even while I sit and read my mother's letter there are bursts of activity on all sides, as if it were firecracker day in the hearts of Parisians. This exact moment, for example, Gaston is leaning his elbows on the marble counter he is so proud of arguing with the butcher about the quality of his *pâté*, the latest political *scandale*, and the fidelity of his dog. Although it is not yet nine in the morning, and the sun is still yellow and clean like a baby egg in the pale blue sky, the discussion at the counter has taken on great urgency. Coffee and various distilled products are being gulped down, cigarettes are being emphatically ground to shreds with twisting, bayonet-like movements. The butcher, in fact, was reputed to be a sadist during the war, a resistance fighter who was himself tortured on many occasions. Even now, at seventy years old, he makes a terrifying sight. Gaston, much younger, buzzes about him like a puffy mosquito labouring to find an exposed vein in the hide of an elephant.

Around the butcher's van, illegally parked in the middle of the street, other vehicles are screeching, cursing, coming within millimetres of total demolition. And surrounding the butcher himself are the various hangers-on, connoisseurs of nothing, over-tired hookers and streetcleaners who make up the early morning clientele of Café Le Dog. A bit to one side is Marie, demurely dunking croissants into her bowl of hot milk.

Only I am sitting down at a table. I and a few students who don't count, bending over their books. After last night, what am I doing here so early in the morning? Am I so addicted to the sounds of the gutters being washed out at dawn, the peculiar kitchen-like smell of early morning Paris, that I have decided to forego sleep? Has Marie, as a result of our little disaster, left me with the task of writing to my own mother? Am I returning to the scene of the crime to make sure that I am still welcome here, my only home? François Mauriac once said of André Gide that his immorality was merely unforgivable; his truly damning sin was to boast of it in public. That sentiment, no doubt, explains why Mauriac retired from the writing of novels and turned his teacherly attentions to composing the memoirs of his sanctimonious life. In his attack on Gide, he even went so far as to include a chapter saying that Gide's wife was a saint for having put up with him; a saint and a virgin.

Marie, alas, is neither. But she did once say to me that she allowed men access to her body only because it was a crime to deny the one small pleasure she was in a position to give. An old song.

"What about your pleasure?" I asked her.

"That is my own affair."

Marie, at the bar, offers her cheeks to be kissed by a new arrival. Just my luck, it is Claude St. Foy, one of those scabrous journalists who make this place their hideout from honest work. Even the dog, his namesake, is put off by him. He shifts his head from its hour-long vigil across my instep and growls softly. Claude, the dog, is the great-great-grandson, approximately speaking, of the canine after whom Café Le Dog was named. The invading Americans christened it thus, as if they had never seen a dog in a restaurant before, and the GI's even made a sign, since replaced and electrified, to hang above the counter. On the sign is a picture of the initial inspiration, a large and fierce Dalmatian with black, piercing eyes and teeth that would frighten a rhinoceros. Claude, alas, is a small, living monument to the dangers of breeding in the street. A diminutive beast that could almost fit in the crook of your arm, he is covered by brown, curly hair except for his face, his feet, and the tip of his tail, all of which are white. His good looks and loyal personality are undermined by the fact that over the years he has become an alcoholic. By noon he begins leaping onto the counter and stealing the customers' drinks, the stronger the better; and at a certain peak point – when he is lubricated but not drunk – he scampers from glass to glass, his pink tongue scooping out the liquid at lightning speed. Even drunk, he never upsets a glass before midnight. After that he gets maudlin, staggering about on all fours, cruising, a sad, doggy look attesting to the tragedies he would be only too delighted to relate.

Today, because summer is coming, Marie wears less clothes than usual. A scoop-necked sailor's jersey, a skirt, high heels that show off her perfect legs. A childhood attack of the pox has left her cheeks looking like a bed of gravel, and the effects of wine have already been mentioned, but otherwise she seems unusually young and beautiful today. Twenty years younger, for example, than she looked only a few hours ago, when she was weeping and spitting insults as if the night would never end.

Marie was born the year after the war. She claims her existence began the day the Americans entered Paris. Like me, she was brought up by her mother. But her father did not die, he merely ran away with a troupe of gypsies. "The war unsettled him," Marie explained. "It made him restless. Also he hated my mother because she – it was a matter of temperament. She was from Paris, he from the south. Anyway, a man with Basque blood is almost a gypsy already. If it weren't for the war he would have left long ago, to tell the truth. My real father is the American army. If they hadn't come to Paris in such a splendid way, my father would never have gotten drunk enough to admit desire for my mother again."

You don't need me to tell you how mysterious are the ways of the heart. Marie's mother, at sixty, is still extraordinarily beautiful. Her fine nose and slate-grey eyes belong also to Marie. But the rest of her features, noble and patrician, are hers alone. Also her creamy, almost transparent complexion, which only a lifetime of abstinence can give. She looks, in brief, like the Mother Superior of an upper-class convent, the kind you can't stop wondering about. In fact I once lived near such a convent in Montreal, and during the summer we climbed trees every day to see if we could catch the nuns sunbathing. Disgusting, but youth is meant to be ridiculous. The convent look is, of course, something Marie has avoided altogether. Yet even in her career as a part-time wife she has always held something back. And I don't mean the pleasure that Marie delights in hiding, because between women and pleasure is a bond invisible to most men. Then what? Perhaps only that little indigestible pebble of fundamental human essence that makes even the most rabid passion choke to death. Or perhaps her heavy exposure to Henry James has caused a set of unpredictable short circuits in her nervous system, some weird syntactic lobotomy that would take a team of psycho-linguists years to unknot.

Despite everything, including her clothes and her smell, Marie is still an attractive woman. She has not only her mother's eyes and nose, but rounded apple cheeks and a smile flawed only slightly by a darkened tooth that should have been replaced by one of her affluent boyfriends. On the other hand, for a woman not yet forty, Marie has let herself slide into some very strange habits. She often talks to herself as she walks, and to see her coming down the street, chattering away with her head wagging back and forth, you would think something more than Henry James had gotten to her. Also she cries too easily; the slightest mean remark sends her into an orgy of tears. Since retiring from sexual commerce with paying customers, she has lost her social tastes altogether: her only friends are her brother, the customers at the *café*, and myself. I am, she claims, the only non-paying client she has ever entertained. But where I stand in Marie's cosmos is unknown to me. In fact, there is that balance between us only too typical of men and women: she understands me perfectly; I find her absolutely opaque.

I was on my third brandy when my mother walked into the Café Le Dog. Forewarned is not forearmed, as they say: I didn't even recognize her. What I saw was a thin old woman, erect, wearing a black coat with a colourful tourist's shawl about her shoulders. She had white hair, lined cheeks, a smear of lipstick on her mouth. Even this I only noticed because before she was through the door Marie had leapt forward to embrace her. Then they sat down at a table and began to weep with happiness while I was still staring at the last line of my mother's letter: *Don't worry about meeting me at the airport. I will come to see you as soon as I have found a suitable hotel.*

They might have sat talking and crying all morning without my recognizing her, but her voice trolled through my mind like a baited hook.

"There you are," my mother said as I joined them, "your wife has been telling me all about you." Then my mother turned away from me and extracted a compact from her purse. She popped it open and looked intently at herself in the mirror. "Do you think I've changed?"

"Only for the better," Marie said quickly.

"Thank you, you're a kind girl, everything I could have hoped for." They were speaking French. It was amazing; my mother's accent was so perfect. The twenty years I had spent in France, she had used to even better effect in the mental home, improving herself. Now my mother reached into her purse again, this time pulling out the last of my poetry books. "I've always wanted your autograph."

In this memoir, more than modesty forbids me giving samples of my poetry. Believe me when I say it is all terrible. So hopeless, in fact, that under the name of Claude St. Foy, I have turned to criticism and make my living writing book reviews for French newspapers. So bitter and vitriolic are my comments that St. Foy's reviews have often been syndicated. Like most journalists, St. Foy is a complete illiterate, so our collaboration is lucky for both of us: between us we make the perfect critic. In fact, our strange star has risen so high that sometimes we even review French books for the *Herald Tribune,* who marvel at St. Foy's fluent command of written English.

But don't take my bitterness as a sign of failure. In fact, the execrable volume my mother had preserved, *Songs of the Seine,* was quite a success. Written in English, it was translated into French before being published by my uncle. I, of course, though under a pseudonym, was the translator. But my picture is on the back, and I am identified as a Canadian.

Writing and translating the book were only the first steps. Next I used St. Foy's name to give the book a scathing attack in *Le Monde,* correctly calling it a pitiable example of neo-structuralist Canadian drivel. Naturally, this brought the book to the attention of the Canadian government, and an English version duly appeared from a small Toronto press. According to the newspapers, it almost won an award, and I was offered a lecture tour of the Canadian West. I declined, the only act of my life that has been tainted with integrity.

This is not to say I failed to benefit from my Canadian notoriety. Taking lecture offer and newspaper clippings in hand, I dressed in my best clothes and Gaston's best *foulard,* and presented myself at the Canadian Cultural Centre. I wished, I said, a small lifetime pension as a distinguished Canadian poet in exile. For bureaucratic reasons they were unable to grant it. But they did offer me a job cleaning the washrooms on Sundays and national holidays. I accepted. It was, in fact, the savings from this employment that I used to send to my mother to make her life easier in the mental home. Of course I never believed she would be released.

"Does Jean-Paul Sartre really come here every day?"

"He died," Marie said.

But my mother's voice had carried and now Claude St. Foy was hovering over us, rubbing his hands like an undertaker.

"You should have told me."

"I didn't want to–"

"I understand," my mother said. She gave me a radiant smile and I felt like a child again; the way I felt the night after my father's funeral when we came back to our apartment and my mother smiled at me and said, "Now, Camille, we must be good to each other. We are all we have."

The first thing we did was to close the door to the bedroom where my father had died. That night and thereafter my mother slept on the couch. She replaced her entire wardrobe, and continued to call me Camille in memory of my father. Even the sheets he had died on remained unchanged until the day, ten years later, that my mother was sent to the mental home. I was left alone. A welfare worker was assigned to me. She opened the door and strode into the bedroom. The window had been left open – my father had died during a heat wave – and now the room was full of cats and birds. Of course we had often heard noises, especially at night, but had been too frightened to investigate. As the welfare worker stood in the doorway to my father's room, I ran out of the apartment and down the stairs to freedom. In a bank account I had three hundred dollars that had been left to me in my father's will. I bought a ticket for Paris and departed by boat the same day. I had my uncle's address, since he wrote to my mother every week, and a well-worn but unautographed copy of Rimbaud's collected poems.

At first drink inflames the brain, but eventually the effect is to scramble it, so that every drinker ends up splashing feebly down the same river of forgetfulness and self-pity. Or perhaps, let's be frank, this is only wishful thinking, and the truth is that I am one of those people who can't hold their liquor.
 By the time I had signed my mother's poems and St. Foy had seated himself at our table, I was exhausted and muddied. Every word had to be dredged up and I couldn't hear what the others were saying. Of course, I didn't want my mother to know what a bad way I was in, so I began telling jokes. Soon St. Foy had taken over and was reciting lurid stories I'd heard a thousand times before. My mother was entranced and Marie was smiling, even at me. Another of our disastrous arguments had obviously melted away, into that undercurrent of oblivion that moved us along from day to day – But no! Here is that talk of darkness again. How sentimental we poets, even failed ones, become at the mere thought of death. Even the demise of animals and vegetables becomes the humus of literature. But life is different. For example, the young GI's, drunk no doubt, who hung Café Le Dog from the ceiling, could not have felt that they were being smothered by the wet blanket of life. And, except in these memoirs or when I am complaining to Marie, neither do I. After all, I am still a Canadian citizen. This, in fact, is my last and only hope, the rock my mind clings to in its most desperate moments. Every week, when I have finished my cleaning tasks at the Cultural Centre, I spend a few hours reading the Help Wanted columns of Canadian newspapers. One day, I still believe, I will see advertised a government job that is suitable for me. And then, God will-

ing, let bygones be bygones. I will take Marie home with me to my native land and, if our vital organs are still functioning, give myself over to honest work and raising children under sanitary conditions.

"Aren't we ever going to go home?" By midnight at Café Le Dog even my mother was beginning to wilt. Marie, it turned out, had known she was coming all along, and had even used the trans-Atlantic telephone to confirm the hour of her arrival.

"I didn't know how to talk to a hotel," my mother said. "You must have an apartment, a room, even a kennel somewhere to sleep in. Take me to it."

"Allow me," St. Foy interrupted. "My wife and I would be delighted to be your hosts. We have a spare bedroom, entirely furnished in authentic furniture."

"Forget it," my mother said. "I never sleep in a house with a strange man, no matter what the excuse."

"But I am practically your own son." He had stuck to her the whole day, such an idiot that he was incapable of realizing that to fall in love with my mother would involve him in a terminal form of incest.

"I'm willing to love you," my mother declared, "and to answer faithfully whatever letters you might send." She stood up.

Only once before had I seen my mother drunk. That was the New Year's Eve before my father died. On that occasion they were both dressed like stars from an old movie: my mother in a long, backless, satin dress, my father in a tuxedo. It was long past midnight when they came in. The neighbour who had been watching me had gone home, but I was lying awake, keeping away the ghosts by listening to country music on the short wave radio. Even from my bed their laughter sounded like the clinking of glasses. I put on my housecoat – as an only child they liked to dress me up like a little adult – and came out to investigate. My father had kicked off his shoes and was slouched in an easy chair, smoking a last cigar. He was a businessman whose fortunes had moved in gigantic cycles – during my life always downwards – but to me he always had the fancy clothes and bay rum aura of a wealthy tycoon. My mother was standing in front of him, her face pink and girlish. She had lifted her dress up to her thighs and was standing on one foot, the other extended like a ballerina's, toe pointed towards the door. When she saw me her eyes opened wide, like doll's eyes, then very slowly her lips parted. "I've been meaning to tell you," she said; and then she toppled over and landed on the floor in an unbreakable sleep. My first book of bad poetry included an unsuccessful sonnet describing this very event; prose, too, fails to convey the heart-stopping pleasure my seven-year-old self felt at being singled out for such an important announcement, even if unmade. Of course, after my father's demise I was chosen all too often, but that is another story.

"Take me somewhere," my mother whispered to me in English. "Quickly."

Having passed the whole day at the same table, drinking brandy in the morning, then switching cautiously to beer for the afternoon before plunging into the celebratory evening bottles of wine, I was in more than my usual fog when we stepped outside. Soon we were walking down Boulevard Raspail – Marie, my mother, myself – the cold April air sweeping us along the sidewalks. We turned into the tiny street where Marie lived, unlocked the door and twisted our way up the stairs to her top floor apartment. Marie switched on the light. She was, you might say, a closet intellectual; or at least her place resembled a closet in which was stored every shred of printed paper that had been generated since Gutenberg's ill-fated inspiration.

"Tell me this is Paris," my mother said.

"This is Paris," said Marie.

"It was a wonderful first day," my mother said. "But I *was* looking forward to meeting Jean-Paul Sartre. Are you sure he's dead?"

"Absolutely," said Marie. "I went to his funeral."

"Then you *were* good friends."

"*Copains.* Really. We were like that." She crossed her fingers, the way she always does when she wants to signal God that she is telling a lie for reasons He would surely understand.

"And he really admired Camille's work?"

"He was devoted."

My mother lay down on Marie's bed. It was covered with layers of the clothes she usually wore, old newspapers and magazines, two ashtrays, and a set of pillows one of her paying lovers had brought her from Japan. But to all this my mother was oblivious. She pulled the mess over herself, willy-nilly, not even taking off her shoes, and lay on her back with her head cushioned on a first edition of *The Golden Bowl.*

"I said to Mme Dufresne that I would come to Paris and see my son Camille. I swore to her that I would speak to him, his friends, his associates, even Jean-Paul Sartre, in their own language whatever it was. I told her I would do all this before my life was over, no matter what."

"Don't die," Marie pleaded.

My mother's lips quavered. "Don't worry," she said. "I didn't come all the way to Paris just to die. I only ask that you watch me sleep. If you do I will last until morning and then you will see that your efforts have not been wasted. My life is only beginning."

"Goodnight, mother," I said.

"Goodnight, Camille. Your father would be proud of you, despite everything."

While my mother slept, Marie and I talked in whispers about our pasts, our hatred of Claude St. Foy, the chance that her brother Gaston might fatally wound himself shaving. Eventually, we lay down on the floor and made love. When it was over I suddenly remembered that my mother had asked us to watch over her at all times. But she was still breathing. In the morning the three of us went to Café Le Dog and took our coffee outside. No one in Paris could have been happier.